cruel
BEAST

USA Today Bestselling Authors

J.L. BECK & S. RENA

Copyright © 2022 by Bleeding Heart Press

Cover Design: C. Hallman

Cover Photographer: Wander Aguiar

Editing: Kelly Allenby

Proofread: Editing for Indies

All rights reserved.

No part of this book may be reproduced in any form or by any electronic or mechanical means, including information storage and retrieval systems, without written permission from the author, except for the use of brief quotations in a book review.

PREFACE

Family. A bond between a group of people who share the same blood. At least, that's how it should be. A father, mother, sister, brother—I have none of that and learned early on that the word means something different for everyone.

While most people are loved and raised to be kind, functioning members of society, I was left fighting for my life as a toddler next to the corpse of my mother by the man who should have nourished me. Samuele Russo—ruthless, tyrant, and DEAD. Of course, he can thank me for that.

My first memory in life is cruelty, and from that moment on, it's become the very essence of my being. All my life, I was tortured by that fact, and now that I've gotten my revenge, it's time I finally fulfill my mother's legacy and take my place as the reigning king of the De Luca dynasty.

BEAST

1
ALICIA

"Please. All I need is a little more time. I promise I'll be able to get the money together. It just won't be right now."

I'd love to say this is my first time inside this office, but it's not. It isn't even the tenth time. By now, my advisor and I are on a first-name basis. That makes it even more painful when he sighs and leans back in his chair after hearing my sob story for nearly the one-hundredth time.

"I'm sorry, Alicia." He shrugs and tosses his pen on the desk. "But there's nothing I can do."

I hold up my folded hands. "John, come on. Please," I beg. "You know what it's been like for me."

"I do because we go through this conversation every time I have to call you in for late tuition payments."

It takes everything inside me not to grit my teeth and roll my eyes. Instead, I make nice because, at the end of the day, I need him. "They cut back my hours at the store," I explain even though I know he doesn't want to hear it. "I could try to get a second job, but then I won't have any time to go to class."

As it is, I barely sleep at night since I hardly have time to study otherwise. I'm practically killing myself to get through college, so I might as well try to pass my classes. Otherwise, what's it all for?

Like always, he is sympathetic, but that's about as far as it goes.

"I understand. I really do. Many of us are going through hardships. It's just the fact of life right now."

I shake my head in frustration. "That's not even mentioning the fact that everything is more expensive now. Tuition has been raised. I don't see how anybody can keep up with this, even people with families paying for them."

He leans forward, folding his hands on a stack of folders. He's a nice guy, a family man with photos of his kids lined up on his desk. I get the sense he doesn't make much in his job—his clothes are always a little worn. And once, I passed a shoe store at the mall and could've sworn he was one of the guys helping customers locate a style in their size. But the store was pretty crowded, so I could have been wrong. Still, it wouldn't shock me to find out he has a second job.

"You aren't the only person going through tough times," he explains in a quieter voice than the one he used before. "And I agree with you; it's startling the way costs seem to rise every year. Inflation's a bitch, too—pardon my language."

Yes, that was one of the reasons they gave me at the store for cutting back hours. It costs more money to ship products to the stores across the country and more to produce them, so they have to save money where they can. That means people like me go bye-bye.

"I do everything I can to locate money for the students assigned to me." He plops a hand on top of a thick stack of file folders. "Here are just some of the people who've passed through my door in the last week alone. Pretty soon, my kids are going to forget what I look like if I keep pulling the kind of hours I've been putting myself through."

I feel sorry for him, but what am I supposed to say? "And are you able to help them?"

"Some. Others have used every last resource at their disposal, but it still isn't enough." He lowers his brow, gazing at me from over the top of his glasses. "Does that sound familiar?"

"Are you trying to guilt-trip me?"

"Of course not." He looks at me like he can't believe I would think such a thing. "I'm just saying there's only so much that can be done. We've been here before, Ms. Gutierrez, and every time we've managed to pull something out of thin air. But a lot of these programs are tapped out now. The grants, all of it. You're going to have to find a way to make up the difference yourself. I'm sorry, but the school has policies in place for a reason."

Policies. Rules. I'm so sick of hearing about them, sick of everybody else getting an extra pass except for me. There are so many other arguments I can make, but I've made them all before. He practically knows my entire life story by now. I'm surprised I didn't get invited to his kids' last birthday party. We spend so much time facing each other across his scarred, scuffed metal desk that we might as well be family.

Speaking of family, I don't have any to fall back on. I don't have anything valuable that I can sell. There are only so many hours in the day, and I doubt I could devote enough of them that anybody would bother hiring me.

His eyes light up, and for a moment, I have hope. "Could you find work someplace else? If they've cut back your hours—"

So much for hope. I shake my head, nauseated more and more with every passing moment. "I've already applied for everything anywhere near campus, but jobs are scarce. Everybody keeps telling me more spots will open after graduation, but what good will that do me now? Besides, the company covers part of my tuition as it is. I'd be in worse shape if I quit."

"I know, it all seems impossible."

"Seems?" I scoff, "No, it is. You're telling me I'm going to be kicked out of school at the end of this semester unless I can pay the rest of my bill, which we both know I can't."

"You won't be kicked out," he reminds me, and while I know he's trying to be nice, the fact that he sounds like he's trying to talk one of his twin toddlers out of doing something foolish only grates on my nerves. "You'll be put on a waitlist, then re-enrolled when you can pay again. And until then, there's one last extension we can apply for, but that's it."

Yes, that's it. I only have to wait until I can afford it. By then, tuition will go up even higher than before, I'm sure. It doesn't help that some of the classes I need for my major are only offered next semester, then not again for a year. This isn't a matter of just waiting until next year. It would be a year and a half at this point. A year and a half of everyone around me moving on and getting ahead while I work some crappy job, scraping nickels together to afford the basics.

There's a knock on the door, and we turn to find the financial office administrator poking her head in. "Your five o'clock is here," she murmurs, offering me an apologetic smile. In other words, it's time for me to go.

"Don't give up hope, Alicia," he says, his brows pinched together in a pained expression as he extends a hand to shake.

I return the gesture robotically, doing it only because it's expected of me. This gets more painful with every passing moment. I know I shouldn't feel ashamed, but I can't help it. I'm a loser, at least in the eyes of the powers that be around here. Just one more pitiful person who can't quite seem to get things right. It's enough to make me want to crawl into a hole and bury myself.

I should walk out of his office with my head held high since it's not like I did anything to get myself in this position. I didn't blow a trust fund or dip into my tuition funds to pay for a lavish trip or anything like that. All I did was commit the crime of being poor, and it seems like there's no shortage of people who want to punish me for it.

When I step outside of the building, I make it a point to take a few deep breaths in hopes of centering myself. Campus has already quieted down a little bit, the way it always does at this time of day. Still, enough people are hanging out, chatting with friends, and listening to music without a care in the world to set my teeth on edge and make frustrated tears threaten to well up in my eyes.

They don't get it. They don't understand how charmed their lives are. Sure, they might have other things weighing them down. Everybody does. But their existence is at least provided for. They can afford their iced coffees, cute clothes, and upgraded phones while I walk around with a phone at least four generations behind.

I've never cared about fitting in, attending parties, or joining clubs and activities. The whole idea of college life never really resonated with me. I'm here to get an education so that I can live a better life in the future. That's all. Not that I don't have any friends, I just don't have time to indulge in fun things the way so many other people do.

"Alicia! Hola, chica!" A voice I know all too well fills my ears.

Life is truly determined to rub this situation in my face. It's not that I didn't like or get along with Elena. Just the opposite. We've gotten along great ever since we met as project partners in a history class last year. She's fun and laid-back and takes no shit from anybody.

It's just that she's exactly the kind of person I was just thinking of. Somebody who never has to worry about anything. She doesn't have to work, so she has plenty of time to hang out and make friends and go to parties. I'm sure if she was the kind of person who joined clubs, she'd be in a ton of those. Whenever we have a few minutes to chat after class, she tells me about how she has to go shopping or how she's got a hair or nail appointment she needs to get to. All I can do is nod and wish I had the kind of life where those were actual problems.

When she reaches me, she frowns, her eyes darting over my face. "What's wrong? Whose ass do I need to kick?"

I blurt out a laugh, but like magic, that single little outburst is all it takes to open the floodgates. The tears that were only threatening to well up now do more than that, spilling onto my cheeks before I can stop them.

"Hey, hey, whatever it is, we'll figure it out. Here, take a seat." Elena places a hand on my shoulder, guiding me toward the nearest bench. "Can I get you anything? Do you need some water?"

I shake my head, embarrassed, searching in my backpack for a tissue. "I'm sorry. This is so dumb. You don't need to be wasting time dealing with me being a blubbering baby."

"Don't do that. You're like the least emotional person I know, which means something shitty must have happened. Now tell me, what's going on?"

"It's embarrassing."

"I said, what's going on?"

Obviously, she's not going to let me get away with this. I have to put my pride aside as much as it hurts. Besides, we're friends—*right?*

"Fine! I can't afford tuition. And they're not going to let me slide like they have before. If I can't make up the difference, I'll be put on a waitlist next semester, and I'll have to wait until next year to finish my classes. I can't do that. I can't waste an entire year that way."

"How much do you need?" she asks without blinking an eye.

"I swear to God, Elena, if you're even considering giving me the money, I will walk away from you right now and never talk to you again."

The way she scowls tells me that's exactly what she was thinking. "You could at least answer my question."

"A few thousand." God, it might as well be a million. "I have no idea how I'm going to make up the difference. I barely have time to sleep as it is, and I just got done telling my advisor no places are hiring around here. So I'm stuck with the shitty hours they're giving me at the store. I don't know what else to do. I'm starting to feel like this was all for nothing."

"Don't say that." She frowns.

I almost laugh. "No offense, but it's easy for you to tell me not to say it. I'm the one who knows how I'm feeling, and right now, it feels like all the money I've spent on tuition and everything else was a waste because I'm not going to end up graduating."

I slide an embarrassed look her way, expecting her to tell me to fuck off or something. She was only trying to be helpful, after all. But all she's doing is staring at me—no, studying me, her lips pursed like she's thinking.

"What?" I finally have to ask. "What are you thinking? I can see the wheels turning in your head."

She grins, but only briefly. "It's just that I thought of something that might help you." She hesitates a little.

"I told you, I'm not—"

"Would you stop talking over me and let me get this out?" she demands, shaking her head. "I was going to say, I think I might have a job for you."

"Oh." I sit up a little straighter, wiping away the last tear. "What is it? I'll do just about anything. I'm that desperate."

"It's not... *conventional*."

Oh god, I better stop her before the shit gets deep. "I don't think I'd be a very good stripper if that's what you're thinking."

She bursts out laughing, which is not exactly what a girl wants to hear at a time like this. It's like she agrees with me or something, and it's only slightly mortifying.

"It's not stripping. In fact, you wouldn't have to take off a stitch of clothing. Though don't even act like you wouldn't make a ton of cash if you shook that ass."

I can't help but blush at the idea of shaking my ass for strangers or even for people I know. "So what is it?"

"First, I need you to remember how much you need this money. And I hope you don't freak out over what I'm about to say." She leans in a little closer, her eyes darting around like she wants to make sure nobody is standing too close to us. "I have a way you could make all the money you need and then some in one night."

I'm starting to get the feeling this isn't a completely legal sort of job. And now I have to wonder exactly where my friend gets all her money. Then I remember beggars can't be choosers, and it's not up to me to judge anybody.

Even though I've walked the straight and narrow my entire

life, I'm willing to break that habit if it means being able to pay for school and having a little money left over. It's been so long since I've had any money for more than the basics.

I ignore the way my hands shake and the thudding of my heart against my ribs. I should turn around, go back to my apartment, and cry my sorrows into a book, but even I know that wouldn't solve my problems. I'm desperate, and that means I'm willing to do anything.

"Whatever it is, I'll do it." I decide before she even has a chance to describe the job. "Just give me the details, and I'll be there."

She smirks like she's just solved all my problems, and I cringe because all I can do is hope I don't end up regretting this or—worse—in jail.

BEAST

2

ENZO

The mansion I've spent the past twenty-five years of my life in is still—silent. And it doesn't help that a storm is brewing on the other side of these walls. No light comes in from the large windows on all sides of the house. The dark clouds can be seen from all angles, and that can only mean something is about to go down.

Bad things happen when nature is upset. Violent rains usually bring darkness and mayhem, at least in my world. It rained the day my grandfather found me, left with a gunshot wound to the chest at the edge of my family's property line. My only friend in life was a stark black Great Dane I called Ghost, and the skies roared and lit up with lightning that night too.

Bracing myself, I walk the halls, my soles slapping against the marbled floors. All the staff has retreated to their quarters for the evening, and the only sound to be heard comes from my grandfather's study at the end of the hall. His voice carries through the hall, and I can tell by his tone that he's angry.

When I breach the threshold, he's sitting behind his oversized desk with men on either side of him. He's been threatened more times than I can count, so he's always kept a guard or two with him. The only other person in the room, aside from my grandfather and his men, is Prince, my mother's bastard nephew. We're close in age, and if I'm being honest, not really that close. But he's family, and as a De Luca, that means everything. Especially when my nonno—*my grandfather*—lost both of his children, leaving behind Prince and myself. So despite our childhood rivalry or the fact we carry different names, we make nice where Grandfather is concerned and watch our backs.

"Unacceptable," Grandfather barks into the phone. "Set up a time—now." He ends the call and slams the device down on the desk. "Imbecille di merda." *Fucking moron.*

He breaks into a coughing fit as he snatches open his drawer and removes a lighter and cigar from the engraved cherrywood box. I eye the case. It was a gift from my mother before she ran off with my father and got herself killed. It's the only thing my grandfather kept of hers, and he guards the damn thing with his life.

A parent should never have favorites, but she was his, just like my brother, Christian, was my father's. Naturally, the love Grandfather had for his daughter spilled onto me—so I guess you can say I'm the current favorite.

When Grandfather stares up at me, his brows knitted together with disappointment, I don't know if it's directed at me or whoever was on the other end of the line. Prince notices and turns to follow our grandfather's gaze. A smirk leaves him the moment his eyes land on the sling around my shoulder.

Prince huffs around a laugh, scratching his temple, not bothering to hide his amusement. "Who kicked your ass?" He juts his chin at my wound.

"A Glock 43X." I snort and grip my elbow to help elevate

some of the pressure from the injury. A bout of rage courses through me, thinking about the fact that Christian got the jump on me.

A part of me is pissed I didn't return the favor, but I get it. If the shoe was on the other foot, and he had kidnapped my bride, I'd have done a lot worse than putting a bullet in his shoulder. But I guess at the same time, I should be somewhat grateful. I did try to kill him and would have killed his darling Sián had she not gotten through to us.

"Ouch," Prince says with a hiss. "Did you at least put one in whoever it was?"

"Sit," Grandfather interrupts, then coughs again before bringing his cigar to his lips and lighting it.

I hate smoking. It's disgusting and reeks like shit. Not to mention it'll fucking kill you. But then again, when you live the life we do, death from lung cancer is the last of your worries.

"Nonno." I greet him while lowering myself in the seat next to my cousin and crossing my ankle over my knee. When I sit back, I wince from the jolt of pain that shoots through my shoulder.

Grandfather exhales, a cloud of smoke blurring my vision, and I dissipate it with a backward wave. But he takes another puff, this time blowing the smoke toward the ceiling.

Renato De Luca, Capo, ruthless ruler and biggest cocaine distributor in all of Italy. He's a hard man and evil when angered and whoever was on the other end of that line did just that.

"He's in a mood," Prince leans in my direction, stating the obvious.

"Clearly," I retort.

I'd bet a million dollars that I know why he's so riled up—

when he's pissed at one of us and when someone fucks with his money. My money's on all of the above.

"Is it done?" Grandfather asks, his tone stern.

Bingo. I know this man better than anyone. My whole life has been spent at his side, learning everything there is to know from him, and that includes his tics. You don't become Sottocapo by being oblivious to the signs right in front of you. But you also don't earn the title without shedding a little blood.

And because avenging my mother was important not to just me but the entire family, he allowed me to have that moment. For years, I'd been obsessed with finding out the truth, and once I finally put all the pieces of the puzzle together, I couldn't think about anything else.

Soon, I'll be sitting right where Renato is, but the way my grandfather saw it is that I'll never be the ruler I'm meant to be if I don't make the man who killed my mother and left me bleeding on the side of the road pay for what he'd done. Even if that man was my father, he shed De Luca blood, so it was only fitting we did the same. And now that I've gotten it out of my system, I can finally become the man Renato raised me to be.

"Samuele Russo is dead, a bullet between his eyes."

We stare at each other for a moment, his gaze pensive and cold.

"And your brother?"

I swallow a breath. "Not going to be a problem."

"Good." He snuffs out his cigar, then uses his eyes to instruct Prince to pour us all a tumbler of whiskey. "Now on to business."

I nod and settle in for the meeting. Prince hands us each a glass of our own and returns to his seat. Things have been in the works to establish a territory in the States, but dealing with my estranged family was something that couldn't wait. And he had been willing to allow me that. It's the only way I could truly focus on the family. Finding out the truth about Inna, my mother, and killing my father had become an obsession, one that I was forced to overcome or risk losing my title as Underboss to Prince.

Grandfather has been grooming me from an early age, and as the years have gone on, he's prepared me to take on more of a leadership role. He says it's time that I earn the name I've been born into, and for that reason alone.

He hasn't figured out yet that Prince and I see the toll this life has taken on him. He's aging, and while still a son of a bitch, he's not nearly as quick as he used to be. Not to mention all of the coughing fits lately.

We haven't found the courage to let him know that we see him, despite how strong he is. And we won't. De Luca men don't do sympathy, and they'll never admit to weakness.

"I'm ready." I bring the glass to my lips, swallowing the contents in one gulp.

Grandfather clears his throat before taking a sip of whiskey. His eyes are dark, sunken as if he hasn't slept in days, and though he's fighting hard to keep a steady hand, the trembling is obvious. He's sick and has been pretending he isn't ailing for some time now.

Knowing how proud he is, I decided to push the thoughts away, shelving them for another conversation. He'll have to confide in us soon enough, but the expression he wears tells me that whatever he summoned us here for is more important.

"I'm sending you to Miami."

With my lips pressed in a straight line, I nod. "The Alvarezes finally came to their senses?"

Prince smirks and leans back in his chair. "A proposito di fottuta ora." *About fucking time.* He rants.

Grandfather ignores his outburst and puts his attention on me. "No. That's why I'm sending you two."

Prince perks up as he always does anytime he's given the chance to prove himself. It doesn't fall very far from the family tree if you ask me. The sight of blood is exciting, and Prince lives for the chance to draw it. He's our enforcer, and I'd be lying if I said he wasn't damn good at it.

"Alvarez has agreed to meet but may need a little convincing." He pauses for a beat. "Your job will be to scope things out, set up the initial meeting, and ensure a deal is made."

"Not a problem," I add, accepting the challenge.

"Enzo." His tone is clipped and serious. "This needs to go off without a hitch. An agreement needs to be made before returning to Italy. Do you understand?" He stares at me, his gaze just as cold and accusatory as his tone, almost as if he's warning me not to fuck up.

A wave of resentment threatens to wash over me, but a deep breath settles the thoughts before they arise. There's no point. Trust is earned every day with this man, and it's not like I haven't given him hell over the years. The same way I know all there is to know about him, he can read me like a book, too.

"Don't worry. You'll get your deal."

He tips his chin in my direction and then points his sights on Prince. "You're to go with him."

Prince shuffles in his seat, eagerness creeping across his features. He tries to dial it back, but it's too late for that. Grandfather sees it and lets out a heavy sigh.

"What do you need?"

"Routes. The Cubans run most of Miami, and we need to secure an alliance."

"We have routes, too," I remind him.

He shakes his head. "Not as many. And if we aren't careful, we'll lose what we do have. We have the product, and they have the territory. It'll be your job to make sure they realize they need us."

"And how am I supposed to do that? The Alvarezes haven't particularly been our biggest fans."

"Get creative. Make it so they see the value in our families working together."

"And if he doesn't?"

I fix my eyes on him, baiting him for an honest answer. He knows just as much as I do that Josef would rather die than work with us. Over the years, we've found a way to exist, which is a miracle, considering how deep the hate goes with the Alvarezes and the De Lucas. A war that is only simmering under the surface, waiting to explode. The fathers before them managed to silence the beef, all with the promise that we stay out of each other's way. And now we're supposed to work together?

"What are we walking into?" I dare ask.

"Josef is a smart man, and smart men like money. He's also bleeding through it and needs this connection a lot more than we do. The stubborn asshole has agreed to meet; you just need to convince him."

"I'll need the research file—give me every piece of evidence you have on him."

Grandfather opens the drawer on his right and removes a manila envelope, slapping it on the desk only inches in front of me. He coughs again, then takes a sip of whiskey as I lean forward, setting my empty tumbler down and picking up the package.

Prince huddles close while I undo the string that binds the

flap close and reach inside. The stack is thick and smooth like photos, and once I dig the files out, I know that I'm right.

"And Enzo."

We stare back at Grandfather simultaneously, waiting for him to continue.

"Make the connection, stay out of trouble, and come right back home," he orders.

I continue to survey his features, a smile tugging at the corners of my mouth. He knows me well indeed, just like he knows my vice of pretty girls on the Miami strip.

"And where's the fun in that," I tease and stand.

Prince follows my lead, taking the envelope when I hand it to him. Grandfather shakes his head, downs the rest of his drink, and waves us off.

"Don't worry, Nonno. I'll be on my best behavior." I turn and head for the exit.

Prince is at my side, reviewing the images. He makes a noise, and I glance in his direction.

"Says here he has a daughter."

"Yeah. Elena's her name, I think," I huff out. "But no one's ever seen her."

"Hm," Prince mutters. "That's probably because she's as ugly as her father."

"Like that would matter to you," I deadpan.

"You say that like it's a bad thing, cousin. Pussy is pussy, and every mouth is fuckable." He shrugs with a grin.

Unfazed by his comment, I snatch the envelope from his grasp and make my way to my quarters to formulate a plan.

"Si alza a mezzogiorno." *Wheels up at noon.* I announce and disappear down the hall.

BEAST

3

ALICIA

This is the stupidest thing I've ever done. Sitting here in this Uber, staring out the window as my surroundings slowly get slummier, is enough to make me question every choice I've ever made in my entire life.

I'm supposed to be a smart person, the girl who's always sensible and reliable. The girl my manager can always count on to arrive at work on time and even pitch in and help when the people from the shift before me didn't finish cleaning their department the way they should have. I'm responsible, kind, and definitely not this person.

What would they think if they saw me now? Looking like a mid-priced hooker on my way to probably the most dangerous part of town? All alone, on top of everything else? Oh, and at night. The cherry on top is the inky darkness the driver navigates as we roll down streets that were smooth only a few blocks ago but now are full of cracks and potholes.

Even he thinks this is a shitty idea, and he doesn't know

the half of what will happen. "No offense, miss, but are you sure you want to be down here all by yourself, especially at this time of night?" He doesn't bother to hide the way he cranes his neck a little, like he wants to see all of me in the rearview mirror.

"I'm sure I'll be fine," I chirp, smiling with my teeth the way I do at work sometimes. When the customer in front of me has shredded my last nerve after an already crazy day. Knowing that, with my luck, even the slightest rudeness would end up getting me written up—or worse. Because that's how my life goes. Other people have leeway to maybe make a mistake or two, but not me. That's never been the case.

All the more reason to accept an insane job like this one, you idiot.

My insides are all fluttery, and I can't stop shaking my foot back and forth. Who am I kidding? I'll probably end up getting nabbed by the cops. For all I know, this could be some undercover sting operation. What if Elena set me up for this because she knows—the way I now know, at least a little bit—how dishonest her family is?

Granted, she didn't exactly use those words, but it was pretty close.

"I'm going to tell you a secret," she continued on the bench outside the administration building. *"Sometimes my family does... things that aren't exactly legal. And when I need a little money, sometimes I'll do my uncle a favor, and he'll give me cash for it."*

"What kind of favor?" I asked, tensing up.

"It's super easy, I promise. You just take a package from a specific location and deliver it someplace else. It's really a no-brainer, and there's, like, no chance of getting in trouble."

No chance? If somebody is willing to pay twenty grand for this delivery, I have a hard time believing this is all safe. Obviously, it's worth a lot more money to somebody, which tells me it has to be drugs or something like that. I mean, she told me to bring the biggest purse I own, and even then, exactly how much could I fit inside? No, drugs are the only thing that makes sense. Small package, big profits.

But even knowing what I'm more than likely about to transport isn't enough to make me change my mind. Because I would do just about anything to make twenty thousand bucks in a single night. Hell, I might even have gone back on my nervousness about stripping if that sort of money was in the mix.

No matter how many times I remind myself how easy this is supposed to be, I can't calm my nerves. I turn my attention to the checklist Elena rattled off once I confirmed that I would indeed take this job.

Short, tight dress.

Apparently, the place I have to go to for the drop-off has a dress code or something. She said it's best to dress this way to fit in, but if anything, I feel like I'll stand out. The sleeveless black dress I'm wearing fits the bill. It's kind of old, and I've gained a little bit of weight since the last time I wore it. Too much stress eating cheap carbs. If anything, it looks even better on me now than it did before. My boobs never quite filled out the top the way they do now, and the way it hugs my hips and ass had my driver checking me out as I climbed into the car.

Hair clean, blown out, and styled like you're going on a hot date.

I did that, too, only slightly burning my fingers in the process. But now my dark hair hangs over both shoulders in big, soft waves made bigger thanks to the hairspray I used way too much of. It's been a long time since I've had an excuse to get dressed up, so I'm a little out of practice.

It doesn't matter. I'm going to blend right in with all the other girls at the club or the bar or wherever it is I'm going to end up. That's the whole point. I have to blend in, avoid attention, and then get the hell out of there while I somehow convince myself this was all worth it. I'm doing this for my future.

I pull the compact mirror from my bag to check out my makeup one last time. Eyeliner and mascara bring out my eyes, while the smoky gray shadow makes them look greener than ever. My lips are full, red like wine. It's a shame I'm not actually going out someplace because I haven't looked this good in a long time. All it took to break out the makeup and brushes was the idea of being able to afford to live.

"Almost there, miss."

I'm not sure if the driver is informing me or warning me, but I murmur my thanks before checking out my list again. The instructions are right there, plain as day, and they couldn't be simpler. The package will be waiting in one of the offices in the warehouse—it should be the only office with lights on. I sure hope that's the case.

The package will be waiting in the top drawer of the desk. All I need to do is take it, put it in my bag, and get it to the location whose address will be on the package. Easy peasy.

I only hope these stupid heels I'm wearing aren't too loud, just in case somebody is still hanging around in there. Elena told me it's usually empty at this time of day, though it's left unlocked specifically for jobs like this.

Man, I wish I didn't have to do this. Even if I get out of the warehouse with no trouble, who's to say everything will be okay when I deliver the package? What if somebody there is surprised and angry when someone other than Elena delivers?

I need to stop asking myself the what-ifs, or I'm going to chicken out before I even get there.

Twenty thousand dollars.

That's what I need to keep in mind. That's why I'm doing this. Elena said she's done it a bunch of times, and she's always come out just fine. She told me to use her name if anybody asks who I am. That everybody knows who she is. I have to wonder if they'll trust me just because I know her, but she seems to think they would. I really hope she's not completely oblivious, being a member of the family and probably getting special treatment because of that. In other words, I hope she wasn't talking out of her ass.

"I can wait," the driver insists when we pull up to the front of the discreet, darkened building.

I kind of want to tell him to stay here, but that was another warning Elena gave me. I can't have the same driver drop me off at the pickup, then take me for delivery. There's too much room for somebody to start asking questions. Three separate Ubers—I'll need a third one to get home after I finish the delivery and collect my money. Good thing this job is paying so much. Otherwise, I might have to complain about how expensive this is turning out to be.

"No, that won't be needed. Thank you, though," I say with another smile, opening the car door and stepping out.

It's creepy how quiet it is, but that's probably just my nerves. I walk quickly but calmly up to the door and turn around just in time to see the Uber driver pulling away. *Here goes nothing.* Just as Elena promised, the door is unlocked.

In front of me, spanning most of the length of the long brick building, is an open area full of crates, boxes, and pallets. I don't have to worry about any of that. What I'm looking for is in one of the offices to the right of the door I just came through. I asked for every detail in advance and made a mental map in my head in hopes of getting in and out as quickly as possible.

Still, I hesitate for a moment once I'm inside, listening hard for any signs of company. I hold my breath and count to ten, but I don't hear anything more than the low hum from the overhead lights. So far, so good.

Three offices down. I count the doors, my heart pounding, my senses heightened. I'm so close. This doesn't have to be any harder than the way Elena described it.

Sure enough, the lights are on in the third office. I could crumble with relief, but there was no time for that. That can wait until I get home. Right now, what I have to do is duck inside the office, open the top drawer and pull out... whatever it is I'm transporting, aka what I think is probably drugs. She didn't describe what the package would look like, but something tells me I'll recognize it when I see it.

It turns out, the drawer is empty except for a small, rectangular package wrapped in brown paper. There's an address taped to the top. I'll have to feed it into the Uber app as soon as I'm out of here, but I'm not going to waste another second in this place. I'd rather be outside, even if outside is pretty sketchy and dangerous-looking.

I tuck the package into my bag, then place a book and my phone on top of it. My hands are still shaking, even though I'm practically home free. Maybe it's because, for once, something's turning out the way it's supposed to. For once, I might come out on top.

But first, I need to get out of here. I look both ways before ducking out of the office, then begin hustling my way back to the door practically on my tiptoes, just in case somebody is nearby.

"Over here."

Shit! Shit, shit, shit!

I'm like a scared rabbit, frozen in place, eyes wide and heart racing faster than a heart ever should. There wasn't supposed to be anybody here! But voices are coming from somewhere ahead of me, in one of the aisles between rows of crates. I'm not sure exactly which one, but I know I'm going to have to pass it on the way to the door. They're bound to see me, whoever they are. I stand in place, holding my breath, afraid they might even hear me breathing.

There are two men with deep voices, though I can't understand exactly what they're saying. It doesn't matter. I duck behind a pallet of boxes held together by plastic wrap before creeping down the length of the row while looking around in a panic, hoping to find a lit-up *Exit* sign somewhere. There's got to be more than one way in and out of here. It's a freaking warehouse. There should be a loading bay somewhere, right?

As I wait like a sitting duck, all I can think is how I could kill Elena for getting me into this mess. What happens if some guy who works here finds me dressed like I am, sneaking around? I could be mistaken for a hooker.

I come to the end of the row, facing another narrow aisle before continuing down the next row of pallets. The voices still seem fairly close—and now, I notice something I didn't before: the sound of their shoes on the floor. They make noise, telling me they aren't working boots with thick rubber soles and more like dress shoes.

Just when I thought I couldn't be any more terrified, it occurs to me these could be bad guys. Dangerous guys. The kind of guys involved with the sort of thing I'm now carrying in my purse.

Fuck.

I think I'm going to be sick. There's no way I'll get through this without puking all over the place.

What if they think I'm stealing from them? Without a doubt, they'll kill me.

There has to be a way out. I move a couple of rows away from the men, closer to where I started, but it doesn't look like any doors are along the far wall. They must be in the back, opposite the entrance I came through. Right now, as scared as I am, it might as well be ten miles away. Forcing a deep breath into my lungs, I try to calm myself.

The only other option is to wait it out, and I don't know how long they'll be here. My thoughts run rampant…what if they're here to do something a lot worse than pick up drugs? Something they wouldn't want witnesses for?

My panic is growing by the second. I need to run. I need to get out.

Especially since it sounds like the men are on the move again, and shit, they're coming closer with every step.

BEAST

4

ENZO

There's nothing quite like doing all the legwork for a big meeting—the research, the planning, developing an idea of how to respond to various questions that might come up—only to be left hanging when the other party doesn't see fit to show.

I can't help but growl at Prince, who's listened to me bitching since we arrived and found ourselves alone. "This is bullshit. Is this how the man starts a relationship with a potential business partner? By leaving him to hang?"

"How much longer should we stay?" Prince leans against a stack of crates, arms folded while I pace.

"How the fuck should I know?" I fire back.

He remains impassive, satisfied to watch me unravel.

"You realize there's no way for us to go back to Nonno and tell him this didn't work out?"

I pause and direct my gaze at him. "He couldn't blame you —us—for this."

"You do know who we're talking about, don't you? Surely, you've learned a thing about the man's temper? If memory serves, you were with me in his study not so long ago, and you've witnessed his wrath on more than one occasion."

He takes this calmly, too, merely shrugging. "If the man didn't see fit to show up, there isn't much you can do. If we push too hard, we run the risk of appearing desperate. And like Renato said, Alvarez needs this much more than we do."

That prick. What's his game? What's he trying to prove? "So help me, if he's hiding somewhere, waiting to see how long I'll take this before walking out, I'll break his neck."

"Who knows? He might have gotten stuck in traffic," he teases.

The look I shoot him is murderous, and he holds up both hands while wearing an expression that's almost apologetic. *Almost.*

"Trying to lighten the mood, is all. It won't do you any good, looking like you're ready to tear someone's head off if the man walked in this very minute. Remember. Never let them see what you're thinking."

The way he talks, I'd think he was the one who spent his formative years learning at our grandfather's side. It wasn't until he, too, was left orphaned when his bastard father was murdered in a deal gone wrong that Renato brought him to live with us.

"You don't need to tell me that. I know how to turn it on and off when need be." I'd be dead a dozen times over by now if I didn't.

When I was a child, I couldn't understand the different masks my grandfather wore and still wears to this day. I couldn't comprehend how he spoke disparagingly or even bitterly about our rivals in the privacy of his study, among his men, then behaved entirely differently to their faces.

He sat me down and explained that lesson to me one day

when I finally blurted out my confusion. I remember him as he was when I was a kid. He seemed to me like the biggest man in the world. Unbeatable, unbreakable, made of steel. When he spoke, I listened—not that he ever gave me much of a choice otherwise. I shudder at the memory of some of the punishments he inflicted when he caught me zoning out or disobeying him.

"We never show the world our faces," he told me at the time, sitting in the study with a cigar between his teeth. *"To each other, yes, because family is all we have. But the rest of the world? We can't afford to let our guard down, not ever. That's when mistakes are made, and lives are lost. One day, when you're sitting at the head of our family, you'll understand the responsibility of so many lives depending on your judgment. Whether or not you can hide your true feelings in a tense situation."*

From that day on, I trained myself to keep my true thoughts and feelings hidden when in the presence of anyone I didn't trust, which essentially means anyone outside my family. I've smiled in the faces of men whose lives I ended moments later and felt nothing when their bodies hit the ground. I've lost not a moment's sleep over it either because my grandfather was right. Family is all we have, and I protect what's mine. Anyone who fucks up badly enough to earn a bullet between the eyes is an enemy of my family.

Yet there's no revealing my thoughts in advance. Does the spider show off its web to the flies it hopes to trap?

In other words, as much as I'd love nothing more than to kick Josef Alvarez's face in for making an ass out of me, I'll be deferential once we're face-to-face. Even overly so.

I mutter a string of colorful Italian phrases once I check my watch. "We've been here an hour." My feet are about to wear grooves into the concrete floor from all this pacing.

"What's the protocol for a situation like this? What's a respectable amount of time before giving up?"

"I don't have the first clue. But something tells me if we waited three hours, Renato would wonder why it wasn't three hours and one minute."

The way he snickers tells me he knows as well as I that it's true. "Try reaching out to him? See if he has any thoughts? Maybe something has changed with Alvarez."

"You don't think he would have told me the moment anything changed?" I shake my head, my anger growing with every step I take. "One big fucking game."

When moments pass without a response from Prince, I look his way to find him staring straight ahead. I follow his gaze, finding nothing but a pallet of boxes wrapped in plastic, compressed into a cube. Is he suddenly interested in small kitchen appliances?

I'm about to ask him that very question when something inside me thinks better of it. It's the pensive expression he wears. He isn't zoned out because of boredom or a lack of any way to calm my temper. He's watching something. The hair on the back of my neck stands on end, and I wonder if Alvarez sent someone after all. Are we being watched? Listened to?

Keeping that in mind, I amend my approach, pulling back a little on the rancor. "When I think of the trouble we went to in order to come out here and how eager Grandfather is to make this work." I rub my hands together, keenly aware of the tightness in my shoulder with every move I make. I didn't want to arrive for a meeting wearing a sling and looking weak. Besides, I hardly need it. So long as I don't get any ideas about lifting weights anytime soon, I should be fine.

"Don't act like you won't make up for it, hunting for pussy."

Even when he speaks to me, he's staring at those boxes. Why? I finally pass him and take a look from the corner of my eye.

Now I see it. Dark hair, the top of someone's head. Someone is hiding behind those boxes. It isn't close-cropped, either, but parted in the center and shining in the light coming from over our heads. A woman? I exchange a glance with Prince to indicate my understanding but keep quiet on it.

"What I do on my time is my business. But it still isn't reason enough to cross an ocean and end up in this humid swamp."

A woman. Why would Alvarez send a woman? Is this another means of throwing us off-balance so he can take the stronger position? Yes, he needs this deal, but I imagine a shrewd one like him would want to take every opportunity he can to get a leg up. No one in his position wants to be perceived as an easy conquest.

"All the more reason for the girls to take their clothes off," Prince muses with the ghost of a grin playing over his mouth. His eyes widen a little, and I look over in time to see the head bobbing slightly, moving away from us.

Without saying a word, we follow its progress.

"There are plenty of naked bitches back home. And fucking them doesn't involve being treated so poorly by someone we only wanted to work out a deal with. Renato's information must have been wrong. Alvarez isn't dedicated to this. He must've been fishing to find out whether we were."

She darts across an aisle formed by the rows of boxes, and Prince takes off jogging, his feet light, nearly silent. Part of the job is learning how to move without making a sound. I cut to the left and wait, peering around the corner, watching a girl in a short, tight dress teeter around on high heels. I can't pretend observing her tight little ass is a hardship. It sticks out enticingly thanks to the way she bends over, as if that will help hide her from me.

Is she pleased with herself, thinking she's about to make some great escape? That she's as good as on her way to whoever sent her here to gather intel on us? Sadly for them, she's not going to make it.

Prince rounds the corner at the other end of the row, cutting her off while wearing a grin. "Look who we have here? This must be the daughter nobody's seen."

She looks like a deer caught in the headlights of an oncoming car—paralyzed with fear. After a second, she falls back and attempts to turn on her heels, but Prince is too quick. He takes hold of her, hauling her close to him by her arms. Her shocked gasp is music to my ears.

The sight of her is another story. This is the daughter Alvarez has hidden from the world? It makes sense since I would never let her out of my sight if she belonged to me. Not with a face like hers—certainly not with a body like the one now wriggling against Prince as she wastes energy trying to free herself. Her green eyes pull me in, bright and blazing with what I can only imagine is fear.

"Don't you know better than to sneak around while men are doing business?" I ask before taking her from Prince and pulling her close to me. Her crimson lips part to allow for the short, quick breaths that now hit my face.

"Maybe she got lost on her way to a party," Prince suggests. "Unless this is the sort of thing women wear while visiting warehouses here in the States."

"Is that it?" I ask, grinning down at her. "Do your warehouses have dress codes?"

Her eyes are as wide as saucers, and her dark brown hair flows like a soft curtain with every move she makes. And every time that curtain sways, I catch the scent of her perfume. It's intoxicating, reaching my cock in an instant and causing it to twitch in anticipation. I want her. *Now.* Hard and fast.

"Please," she whispers. "Don't hurt me."

She couldn't have chosen anything sweeter to say. Now my cock threatens to go hard at the recognition of her fear. I hold this girl's life in my hands. Even if killing her is off the menu, thanks to her connection to Alvarez, she doesn't know that. Not if the rapid fluttering of the pulse in her throat is any indication.

"Why shouldn't I?" I counter, thrilling at the tiny breath she sucks in when my fingers press into her arms. "You're the one we discovered sneaking around the location of an important meeting. Did they send you as a first wave of sorts?"

I release one of her arms in favor of pressing my hand to her lower back, pulling her tight against my growing erection. "Or are you the first course? A way for my friend and me to loosen up before we do business?"

"No!" she squeals, which makes me laugh. I'd hate to see her reaction if I told her how much I get off on her fear.

The sound of it leaves her trembling, and yes, that's good. I like that. She's falling apart in my arms, and I want nothing more than to savor it because nobody fucks with me and gets away with it. Every ounce of indignation and rage I've experienced tonight will be visited upon her tenfold.

"What gives you the idea you have any say in this?"

She whimpers at my question, shaking her head, her chin quivering. I could stand here like this all night, playing with her, soaking in her delicious reactions. The image of a puppet dancing on strings flashes before in my mind. I'm the puppet master. She'll do as I say, whatever I say, for however long I want her to.

"What was the plan?" I growl, dropping the playful act. "To listen in and take info back to your old man? Was this his way of gaining an edge over us?"

"I-I don't know what you're talking about." She tries to pull away, and her oversized bag bangs into my hip. Not that the sensation registers much when I'm more interested in her tits rubbing against me. Who allows their daughter out of the house in a dress like this?

"I'm sure you don't. I'm sure you're nothing but an innocent bystander." I exchange a glance with Prince over the top of her head before he leans back to look in both directions near the rear of the warehouse. We aren't far from the loading dock, and the car we picked up at the airport is just beyond it.

"Coast looks clear," he announces. "We'd better get out of here."

"Right." I look down at her again and almost experience a twinge of sympathy that never quite crystalizes. "I'm really sorry about this."

She doesn't have the chance to ask what I mean before Prince strikes her across the back of the head with the butt of his Glock.

BEAST

5
ALICIA

Three thoughts slam into me after I wake, startled and in total darkness.

One, judging by how I'm rocking back and forth and the nauseating stench of exhaust, I'm in the trunk of a car.

Two, Elena never mentioned this part.

Three, my head is pounding like someone bashed me with a shovel. Which wouldn't be far-fetched given what I've found myself a part of.

This can't be the plan, can it? No way. Elena would have told me. Wouldn't she? We aren't exactly best friends or anything like that, but this isn't the kind of situation you throw somebody into unless they're your mortal enemy. I don't think I qualify.

My head pounds the harder I try to think. What if the problem is the fact that I'm not her? I was already worried about that, wasn't I? That it was easy for her to say this is a no-brainer, totally safe, and all that because she's part of the family. Recognized and trusted. I'm none of those things.

Dammit, why didn't I think of that before when it could

have made a difference? No, I was too busy being excited over the idea of making a quick twenty grand and kissing all my problems goodbye. Haven't I learned by now things are never that easy?

And now, I might end up paying for it with my life. Because men capable of knocking a strange, unarmed girl unconscious and throwing her in the trunk of a car probably wouldn't hesitate to commit murder at the drop of a hat.

Especially that one guy who was holding me when the other one knocked me out. Damn, he hit me hard—I can barely turn my head without pain tearing through my skull. Did he really need to knock me out? I'm sure a hand over my mouth would have done the job just fine since both men are big and strong enough to subdue me without hardly trying.

No, that was for their pleasure, I'm sure of it.

There's no question in my mind they'd kill me without blinking. My bladder feels too full all of a sudden, and fear isn't helping anything. I'm going to die tonight, aren't I? I'm going to die, and all because I was stupid enough to think there is any such thing as easy money.

And nobody will care. That's the worst part, the part that brings tears to my eyes as the motion from the car rocks me, almost like I'm being soothed—though it would take a lot more than a rocking motion to soothe me right now. Elena might feel bad for a minute, but probably not much more than that. She'll forget me just like everybody else will. I thought I had more time than this.

Would you get your shit together already? I don't know where that voice in my head is coming from, but it's sharp and no-nonsense, and it goes part of the way toward snapping me out of what was about to dissolve into screaming, weeping panic. I don't have the luxury of that right now. I need to figure out a way to get out of this. There must be a way.

What are the facts?

I'm in a trunk. At least two men know I exist after finding me at that warehouse. Dangerous men—they don't have to shoot me for me to know how dangerous they are. The memory of them grabbing me and being so rough is enough.

I have what's most likely drugs in my bag, which they threw into the trunk with me. I'm almost surprised, though they might already have checked it for a weapon while I was unconscious. Not that I thought to bring one with me. Why would I have made a smart decision like that? Oh right, because I was worried somebody would take it the wrong way if they searched my bag and found a knife or something.

There's a good chance they're doing this because I'm not Elena. I have to keep telling myself that. It could be a simple misunderstanding. And it's not like I stole anything from them. The drugs are still in my bag. I didn't even try to use them. They haven't lost anything. Maybe I can convince them of that? When all else fails, tell the truth.

For all I know, this could be how the drugs get to where they're going. And wherever we're headed right now, it could just as easily be the address I was supposed to go to on my own if I hadn't been discovered. I need to think that way so I don't lose myself to panic or fear. This could all end up being an unfortunate, uncomfortable, but easily amended mistake.

And maybe Santa Claus is real.

The car stops, and I've never been so close to peeing myself in my whole life. I force myself to take a few deep breaths before the trunk opens, and I squint up at the man whose eyes I was looking into when I got hit on the back of the head. The red rear lights wash over his face, bringing to mind the devil himself.

But there's no way the devil was this beautiful. I always heard he was before he was cast into hell, but this guy is something else. Like his face was carved from granite by a master, his sensuous mouth set in a scowl as he gazes down at me. If I saw a picture of him in a magazine, I'd assume he was photoshopped to hell and back.

But he is very real and very angry. So angry, he takes hold and yanks me out of the trunk without warning before setting me on my feet, then grabs my bag and slams the lid shut hard enough to make me flinch. He doesn't say a word, taking me by the arm hard enough that I have to grit my teeth to keep from whimpering in pain.

I keep stumbling in my stupid heels along the way up a gravel path leading to a townhouse. Even when I roll my ankle a little, he doesn't slow down, demanding I keep up with his quick gait. He doesn't even say a word or grunt in acknowledgment, and neither does his friend.

Something tells me this is not where I was supposed to be going. Why did I dress up like this if I was going to somebody's house? Do they think I'm really a prostitute and we're going to have a private party? Oh god, just when I thought this couldn't get worse.

Once we're inside, the second man—the one who knocked me out—locks the door behind us. Now I'm alone in a sleek, expensive-looking living room with two men who stare at me like they can't decide how to hurt me first. The one holding me shoves me onto a leather couch and gives me no time to catch my breath before he's leaning over me, crouching low, getting in my face.

I wish I could stop noticing how gorgeous he is. That is not what I need to be thinking about right now. I need to be thinking about survival. Besides, what difference does it make how gorgeous he is? This is a very dangerous man.

His gaze moves over me, and I wait, holding my breath while he studies me closely. There's no telling from his expression what he thinks—it's cold, hard, and maybe that's all I need to know.

"What's your name?" he asks in a deep voice.

Shit. I can't tell him the truth. He might be able to find me if and when he ever lets me go. I search frantically for something to say and finally land on the only other name that keeps popping up in my head. She told me I could use it, right? I doubt she meant it this way, but I'm trying to save my own ass here.

"Elena," I whisper.

"Elena." It flows off his tongue like barbed honey. Now I find myself wishing I could hear him say my actual name—which is maybe the craziest thing of all. Now is not the time to let my hormones get in the way. "And what were you doing at the warehouse tonight, Elena?"

Why lie? All it would take is searching my bag, which his friend is currently holding, to figure things out. And for all I know, they've already been through it, and this is a way of messing with me.

"I was picking up a package." I squirm.

"And what kind of package would that be?"

I can't take my eyes off his sensuous mouth, the way it moves when he speaks. What I need to do is pay more attention to his language and the dangerously dark tone in his voice, like a snake biding its time before it strikes.

"I don't know. Honestly, I only knew there was a package

that needed to be dropped off someplace else. I didn't get any details, I swear."

He stands up straighter, towering over me while I cower in place. It's no use pretending I'm not scared shitless—for all I know, this is all an act to freak me out. If I don't play along, it may piss them off even more.

His eyes darken as his pupils dilate while he rakes over my body. He likes what he sees. I'm torn between wanting to cover myself with my arms and hands and wanting to show him everything he's interested in exploring. What is wrong with me?

"You're not dressed like somebody picking up a package."

"This is how they told me to dress. I swear to God, every word is true."

"And who exactly told you to dress that way? Give me a name."

"I never got a name," I lie, considering I just told him her name as my own.

He folds his thick arms, his biceps bulging against his sleeves. "So let me get this straight. You accepted this job sight unseen, with no knowledge of what you were picking up or where you were going, without even learning the name of the person who assigned it to you? Is that what you're telling me, Elena?"

"Yes. I need the money, that's all." My gaze darts back and forth between him and his friend, but neither of them seems particularly moved. "For school. I have to pay my tuition. They told me I could make a lot of money tonight, so I accepted the job. I've never done anything like this before."

"Right." He takes the bag from his friend, then starts rifling through it.

I know better than to expect him to ask permission, of

course, but it still doesn't exactly make me feel good, having a stranger paw through my stuff. His friend watches me, standing close, sneering when I dare glance his way.

"Here it is." He pulls out the paper-wrapped package and drops the bag on the floor, bending over the coffee table and unwrapping the bundle after examining the address and label on the front.

I realize I'm holding my breath, curious about what's inside. I'm not surprised to find a plastic-wrapped package of white powder. It's almost disappointing.

He withdraws a switchblade from his back pocket—I wasn't expecting that—and flips it open before cutting a tiny slit in the plastic, then withdrawing a bit of the powder using the tip of the knife. I stare, transfixed, as he places a little pinch of the powder on his tongue, frowning like he's trying to figure out what he just ingested.

When his attention snaps back to me with no warning, I sit up a little straighter like a kid who got caught daydreaming in class. Though I doubt my teacher would have killed me for something like that.

"What is this?"

I shake my head frantically even though it hurts like hell. "I swear, I have no idea. I told you. They didn't tell me what I was picking up, only that it was a package, and they told me where I could find it. That is all I know."

Again, he brings to mind a snake when he lunges at me all at once, pressing me against the back of the couch before wrapping a hand around my throat. The pressure causes my air to cut off and my eyes to bulge.

Leaning into my ear, he says, "I'm going to ask you again, Elena. What is in that package?"

How am I supposed to answer when I can't even breathe? I

feel the pressure building in my head, and my lungs are starting to burn with the need for air. I open my mouth, but all that comes out is a gargling noise—and to my horror, he smiles at the sound.

But he also lets up a little. All the color floods back into the world as I gulp in a grateful breath, then another.

"Now. What's in the package? Exactly what is that product?"

My heart sinks with dismay, unlike anything I've ever felt. I thought things were bad when I couldn't pay my tuition? What a joke. "I'm so sorry, but I can't help you. I would if I could," I quickly add.

But he only shakes his head, his scowl deepening into something closer to a snarl. He squeezes harder, and again there's nothing to do but hope he'll let go before it's too late. I slap weakly at his hand, which only makes him take both of my wrists in the other one and squeeze them until my bones grind together and tears roll down my cheeks.

"You're trying my patience," he whispers, and his face is starting to get a little blurry.

I have to breathe. I need to breathe!

But then he eases back some, and I sip air through a thin straw while my head swims. Our eyes meet for the briefest of moments, but it's long enough for something to throb inside me. It has to be the way my head is all foggy now, that's all. I'm losing it.

"You expect me to believe that your father sent you to the very warehouse he was supposed to be meeting me, dressed like a two-bit hooker while carrying a brick of cocaine? I don't know much about Josef Alvarez, but this doesn't seem like him. What does he expect by sending you in his place?"

I shake my head, narrowing my eyes in confusion. But

then, a past conversation resurfaces. I remember Elena telling me that she and one of her cousins shared a name. Something about all the daughters being named after their abuela.

Is that who her cousin is—the daughter of the man who I was supposed to be working for?

"Hm?" he asks when I don't say a word.

How can I? I'm speechless, and this quick job just got ten times more complicated.

Taking my silence as an answer, he says, "That's okay. You'll have another chance to give me what I want." His eyes narrow as his grip begins to tighten, and my heart races faster, harder than ever.

Although, right now, I'm not sure why—is it the fear, or is it the way my pussy is starting to moisten? I'm so ashamed. At least there's no way either of the men could know.

Though they would if they put their hands on me down there. If this dark monster took his hand from my throat and slipped it inside my panties, he'd be able to tell right away how I really feel about this little game he's playing. All the thought does is make me wetter.

I tense up all over when he squeezes harder than before, my head is pounding, and I hear my heartbeat in my ears, each beat slower than the last. He has my life in his hands, and he knows it.

And he likes it.

What's worse, so do I.

He leans in close, examining me like he'd be able to see if I'm lying. All I can do is fight to hold on for as long as I can until everything goes gray and a rattling noise comes out of my mouth without me trying.

He throws me aside, leaving me slumped over, gagging, coughing, and rubbing my throat. A swipe at my wet cheeks leaves my hand streaked with eye makeup. I must look like a total disaster.

But when I sneak a glance toward the man who almost killed me, he's smiling in a way that tells me he likes what he sees. And all I know is that if I want to stay alive, my only option might be to remain Elena.

BEAST

6

ENZO

"Are you hungry?" I munch on a piece of toast, gazing across the breakfast table toward the woman who has sat in a chair all night, her arms bound behind her back. Her head sags with exhaustion, and I'm sure by now she must be sore, especially after being stuck in the same position for hours.

Damned if she's not holding on tight to the same story she told last night. This whole innocent act is already wearing thin. It seems she expects me to—or wants me to rather—overlook the drugs I found in her bag bearing the Marielito stamp. Why in the hell would she have them without knowing what they are?

More than anything, I need to know. I've never been so much as a recreational user of cocaine, but I've tested it more than once while quality-checking our product shipments. What I placed on my tongue last night was like nothing I've experienced before. Somehow, the man has gotten his hands on a unique and potentially powerful product. And we need to know how. I'm here to broker a deal, one that will be royally fucked if he has indeed found a new supplier.

But he left it in her hands, this supposedly innocent, clueless girl? I'm insulted that she would imagine her pitiful excuses believable. No way would he allow her to transport something this special if he didn't know she could be trusted.

Yet to hear her tell it, she's nothing but an innocent bystander. Is that what Alvarez thinks of me? That I'm some rube, who would be easily tricked into believing such an obvious lie? She's lucky I don't take my bitterness out on her here and now, making everything that happened last night seem like child's play in comparison.

I take another bite of toast, noting the way her eyes follow my movements. She's hungry. "You're more than welcome to share some of this with me."

She lifts her chin but remains silent, the stubborn thing. I almost admire her for it.

"Suit yourself," I murmur and take another bite.

It isn't long before my phone rings. I've been expecting this call. He's not going to be happy—and I'll be damned if I mention the drugs in her presence. I tucked them away in my room last night for safekeeping. She doesn't need to hear my theories about them.

"It took longer than I expected to hear from you," I murmur in greeting.

As always, Grandfather wastes no time with niceties. "Is it done?"

This is going to be tricky. Keeping her from him. He wouldn't like this, finding out I've gone behind his back and made such a move. He also wouldn't understand. I'm not certain I do, come to think of it. All I know is, there was no way I could let her go.

"Not exactly."

"What does that mean?"

There's no ignoring the sharpness in his voice. No matter what the years have done to him, how they've grayed his hair or wrinkled his skin, his voice still reminds me of the cracking of a whip at times like this.

"It means Prince and I waited at the warehouse for more than an hour, to no avail. He never showed."

"And you were in the right place?"

I bristle at the question. "Do you have that little faith in me? Why send me here if you feel a question like that is necessary?"

"Now, now. Don't turn bitch on me. Since when do you take things so personally?"

I grind my teeth together. "It was the correct location, at the correct time. We were twenty minutes early, in fact."

He grumbles to himself. "I'll reach out to his people. The goal here is to set a meeting between myself and Alvarez in the next week, so I'll need you to ensure the path is smooth."

My gaze hits the girl staring at me. "You're flying in?" That will complicate things.

"That is the plan. And now this mishap has set me back."

"I'm sure he'll have an excuse." I eye Elena, who is still staring daggers my way. "But all is not lost."

"Meaning?"

"Meaning we picked up something interesting at the warehouse. I'll be checking into it, doing a little digging," I say with my eyes still trained on her.

Try all she wants, she can't hide the recognition of what lies beneath what could have been an innocent statement. I let my gaze trail her scared frame, taking in her features. She is gorgeous, I'll give her that. And that little ass dress she's wearing is all too tempting.

Slender yet curvy in all the right places. Long hair that flows over her shoulders, and despite how disheveled it is from her being hit and stuffed in a trunk, it still looks near perfect. Lips so full and pouty, I wonder how they would feel wrapped around me. Legs so long, I can already feel them around my waist drawing me deeper.

I imagine all the things I could do to her tight little body. I picture all the ways I can bend, fuck, and suck her. And now, all I wonder is if her pussy is as tight as her frame and as sweet as the fear in her eyes.

I run my palm down the front of my slacks, gripping my growing erection. Elena follows my movements, but she doesn't exactly squirm or cower as a girl afraid would. Not at first, she doesn't. It isn't until her eyes meet mine that she acts as she should, shuffling against her restraints and attempting to avoid my stare.

"What would that be?" Renato asks, breaking my concentration.

I stand straight, no longer covering my semi-hard-on from her. "I can tell you more about it later. Now isn't the best time."

Buona fortuna con quello, Micetta. *Good luck with that, kitten.*

"Very well. I'm not in the mood to play games. Do what you need to do to make this work. I will reach out once I get word of another meeting."

I end the call and set the phone down slowly, knowing sweet little Elena is crawling out of her skin, wanting to know what we discussed. Wanting to know what this means for her?

But I can guarantee she only thinks she wants to know. When she finds out, she'll wish she never had.

"Tell me something." I take my time spreading jam on another piece of toast, knowing it has to drive her crazy. Drawing the tension out so she'll be more likely to blurt out answers to my questions, if only to make this stop. "And I want the truth. Don't give me any more of your bullshit pretenses."

"They aren't pretenses." Her voice is hoarse thanks to the fact she's been given no water since arriving.

She'll break soon enough.

"Yes, I'm sure."

Is it my imagination, or does she growl softly at me? I have to give her credit for her spirit. She's entirely under my control with no hope of escape, but she's still feisty.

"Why were you at the warehouse last night? All I want is the truth. Let's face it. Your family left you vulnerable. Why would you go out of your way to shield them now?"

"What difference does it make what I tell you? You aren't going to believe me."

"I don't know that I would go that far. I can be a very understanding person when given the opportunity."

"I'm sure. But you also refuse to listen to the truth when it isn't the truth you want to hear."

"You are determined to irritate me, aren't you? I'm trying to be your friend here." I take a bite of the toast and inch a little closer to her.

"Do friends tie friends to chairs in your world? Sorry, but I can't believe that." She tries to move her arms as if illustrating her point.

"What was that about not believing the truth when it's what you don't want to hear?" I taunt, now only centimeters away.

I hold the half-eaten piece of bread toward her mouth, but she turns her face away, her jaw twitching. Not so much fun when she's caught in her own bullshit.

Trying another tactic, I ask, "Why did your father decide not to show up for that meeting? My family is sincere in reaching out to create an alliance, but that's not possible if he's acting in bad faith. What can we do to fix this?"

"I don't have the slightest idea," she seethes.

"Is there a way I could reach out to him? Get through to him?"

"I'm telling you the honest truth. I don't know."

"Do you know anything at all?" I snap, tossing the toast across the room, the sound of it scraping softly against the hardwood floors.

Elena winces but remains silent, staring at the tabletop rather than me. She doesn't want to play nice? That's fine. She'll soon wish she had.

I round the front of her and lunge forward until she has no choice but to look at me. She draws a quick, sharp breath, sitting up straighter at my movement. Yes, this is better; this is what I wanted. To watch her resolve fade away. She can pretend to be tough and loyal to her family all she wants when there is a table between us.

It's another story now. Once my hands are on her, all bets are off. I doubt she's forgotten the way I manipulated her last night—the faint bruising around her throat tells me it would be impossible to forget.

"Here's the thing, Elena."

She flinches every time I use her name, which for some reason, excites me a little. Bringing my hand to her neck, I run the back of two fingers along her collarbone, tracing the bruises I left behind. She shies away even though it's pointless. She's tied and bound, completely at my mercy.

"I appreciate your loyalty to your family. I do. That's the first and most important principle for people like us, isn't it? Family above all else. But I'm sure you must know there's a limit to that. No one could blame you if you smartened up and saw how useless it is to deny me. I'm going to give you the chance to help yourself here." I pause, kneeling in front of her, bringing myself eye level with her center. The front of her dress has ridden up her thighs from all the squirming, her bright pink panties visible to me.

The need shouldn't burn so strongly within me, but it does, and before she knows what's happening, I yank the chair closer, its legs scratching the floor loudly.

"Ah," she shrieks, her voice seemingly caught in her throat. "Please, no," she pleads.

Ignoring her cries, I touch her inner thigh, and she fights to close her legs to keep me away. I jerk them apart, my focus only on the seat of her underwear. A smile stretches across my face when I spot the slightest hint of wetness long since dried up.

Her skin is soft under my touch as I make my way closer to her sex. And when I trace my thumb over the damp spot, her body shudders. I lean forward, bury my face in her crotch and inhale her scent, locking it to memory. My dick strains against the underside of my zipper, but I will myself to calm, mentally promising myself that the day will come when I get to play in her pretty little pussy, but right now, it'll have to wait.

It isn't lost on me that the moment I pressed my face to her pussy, the fight in her faded just a bit. The recollection brings another grin to my face, but I stifle it before it festers fully.

She whimpers when I get to my feet, reach around, take

the back of her chair, and turn it so she's facing away from the table. Her already huge, fear-filled eyes widen farther when I pull up a chair of my own and place it in front of her, setting it down backward and straddling it with my arms wrapped around the back.

"Tell me what I want to know, and I'll take it easy on you. You have my word. I won't hurt you..." This is her last shot. If she denies me, she'll end up wishing like hell she hadn't. "It's up to you." I rest my chin on the chair, never breaking eye contact while reaching into my back pocket to withdraw a switchblade.

She lets out another whimper, and every muscle in her body tenses at the sight of it once it's visible. "What are you doing?"

"Having a conversation. What does it look like?" It's delicious, her fear. I can almost taste it, and it only makes me want more. I'm a starving man in front of a buffet, wanting to gorge himself until he gets sick. Though I doubt I would ever get sick of her reactions, so predictable yet still so sweet.

"I honestly don't know what you want. I don't know anything."

"That's still the story you're going with, huh?" I don't know if I admire her now or hate her for making this so damn difficult. Why is she covering for this asshole? He sent her into the lion's den and hasn't bothered reaching out to reclaim her. Can't she see that? She doesn't strike me as stupid. Brainwashed maybe but not stupid.

I reach out slowly, the tip of the blade gleaming in the sunlight streaming through the windows. It's a beautiful sight made even more beautiful when I touch the tip to her bare thigh, pressing in slightly. Her flesh is creamy smooth, and I can imagine it painted red. Oh, what a sight that would be.

"Please, don't hurt me," she whispers, trembling now.

"Careful," I warn. "Move too much, and I'm not sure what will happen. I'd hate to pierce this smooth skin of yours."

"I don't know what you want."

"You know exactly what I want," I growl, tracing a line along her thigh, reaching the hem of her dress and easing it up a bit at a time. "And I'm not a man who takes well to disappointment. It could be that I'll have to satisfy myself in other ways."

She squeezes her eyes shut, and a tear leaks from both, trickling down her cheeks. Her chin quivers, and a tiny whimper squeaks out of her, and oh fuck, that's nice. Too nice.

"You can make this end, you know. It's up to you. All you have to do is tell me what I want to know."

Her whimper is louder this time.

"What's it going to take? What do I have to do to make you understand this doesn't end until you give me what I want? Do I have to cut this dress from your body? Believe me, it would be no hardship. Not for me, at least. You might not like it very much."

"Don't," she whispers, fresh tears overflowing and ruining her eye makeup further. My cock twitches, and the beast she brings out, growls in appreciation.

"Did your father never tell you about reciprocity? See, you can't make demands or beg me for something and expect me to fall in line when you refuse to offer something in return."

"I have nothing to offer," she squeaks.

"Bullshit," I bark, thrilling at the way she jumps at the sudden change.

I stand and kick the chair aside, making her duck her head and cringe and weep. No doubt she thinks this will make me pity her when all it does is drive me onward, leaving me wondering what else I can frighten her into. I crouch before her, leaning in close, craning my neck to get in her face no matter how she tries to turn it away.

"Elena, Elena," I croon, shaking my head and clicking my tongue in mock disappointment. "So much potential. We could have a lot of fun together, you and I." When my hands land on the rope holding her in place, she jumps, pressing herself against the back of the chair. I run my hands over her arms, up to her shoulders, and back down again, noting the goose bumps pebbling her tawny skin and the almost violent way she shakes.

"Now, I'll have to have fun all by myself, and I don't think you're going to like it very much." I touch her cheek, tracing the line of her jaw with the backs of my fingers before letting them trail down over her chest and between her luscious tits while she shudders.

"I think my name would look good right here." I trace the letters slowly with my blade, leaving faint pink marks across her heaving chest. "E... N... Z... O," I recite the spelling, taunting her as I do.

Her quiet tears have turned to weeping, and her shoulders shake from the effort. I lean in and touch my tongue to one of them, catching it before it can drip off her chin.

"Delicious," I whisper, reveling in her disgust. All that does is make me lick the length of her cheek, catching the saltiness on my tongue. This is the daughter of one of the most feared marielitos in our world? It didn't take much to break her.

Yet have I broken her if she still refuses to give me what I want? The question grates on my nerves, though not as much as the electric shock that runs through me when our eyes meet. I see her tears, her silent pleading. Her fear. Her pain.

And something else. Something beneath all of it, something I almost recognize because I feel it churning deep in my gut. Excitement? Anticipation? Could that be possible? No, I'm imagining it to give myself an excuse for pushing her harder.

It's bad enough I'm hard as a rock, thanks to her whimpering and squirming. I don't need to imagine her enjoying this on top of it.

BEAST

7

ALICIA

"*D*on't even think about trying any shit in here." He throws me into a small bedroom hard enough to make me stumble and fall against the bed. He leaves a bottle of water and a protein bar on the nightstand while I shrink away from him, hoping he won't hurt me. "My patience is already thin as it is."

This is him when he's being patient?

Turning his back to me, he walks out and slams the door. The sharp click of the lock tells me everything else I need to know.

I'm trapped. In this room, in this house, with these men. This man, who welcomed himself to touch me without my permission, made me cry and licked my tears. I knew there had to be something wrong with him before then, but that was beyond my wildest nightmares.

Still, locked in is better than tied up, I guess. It's not like I expect him to let me wander freely, anyway. But something is chilling about knowing how few options I have.

I've got to find a way out of this. If the man is not going to listen to reason, I'm going to have to resort to something else.

But who am I kidding? He's too strong—the way he threw me around like a rag doll just now is enough of a reminder of that.

And he's cruel. Fucked in the head, completely. If he catches me trying to escape, what he's done to me so far will look like nothing. I'm sure of it.

I have to try. This is only going to get worse. And if I can't use brute strength, I'll have to find something to defend myself with.

At least it's a way to pass the time, searching the room from top to bottom. It's not a big room, and there isn't a lot of furniture. A bed, nightstand, and small dresser. There's a window, so at least I don't feel quite so much like I'm in a jail cell, but it's high up on the wall, near the ceiling. No hope of opening it to escape, though I do try a few times to hop up and grab the sill. It's beyond my reach, though.

I go back to searching, crawling under the bed, opening the nightstand and dresser. They're empty and solidly built. There isn't even the hope of breaking one of the drawers down and using the wood to bludgeon somebody. I'm even desperate enough that I lift the mattress to look underneath, though I'm not sure what I'm hoping to find. A hidden knife? Maybe a gun?

Finally, heartsick and exhausted, I sit on the bed and hold my head in my hands. What am I going to do? How am I going to get out of this?

Enzo—that's his name. Why is he doing this to me? He gets off on it, that much is obvious. He enjoys watching me suffer. I don't even know this guy, but he takes morbid delight in tormenting me. I touch my cheeks where he licked away my tears. It was revolting.

So why did it make my heart flutter? Not to mention the fluttering down below. Wasn't it bad enough that I got wet last night? It's like my body has a mind of its own. Is it a stress reaction? I'm going to call it that because I don't like thinking about what this says about me, the kind of person I am. Who gets wet when a psychotic stranger threatens them with a knife? And he knows it too. He could sense it. I just know he could.

The very thought makes me ashamed of myself. I'm trembling as I lie down—at least I'm able to do this and take the tiniest bit of comfort in the situation. The bed is firm, and the blankets are clean, so at least a little something is going my way.

Is he going to kill me? I curl into a ball at the thought, like that's going to do anything to help me. Why even bother asking myself that question anyway? Obviously, that's what he's going to do. Eventually, he'll figure out I don't know anything about his world or anybody in it. He'll either kill me to shut me up, or he'll do it because he's frustrated with himself for making the mistake of thinking I'm anybody special. Why is it so hard for him to accept that I'm nobody?

Maybe that's because I was stupid enough to give him Elena's name. I should have just told him the truth, then he would have let me go. He would have realized that I'm not lying and free me. As soon as the idea forms in my mind, I push it away. Yeah, fucking right. I may not know about their world, but I know enough to realize that I'm totally fucked. I've seen his face, both of their faces—there's no way he's letting me free, not without death.

My stomach growls, reminding me of that disastrous breakfast and how I didn't get to eat. Not that I didn't want to. I was starving, and with how sparse my finances have been, the last thing I ate was a pack of Ramen noodles. My knee-jerk reaction was to ignore his offer. What's the point of eating, anyway? I'm just going to die here.

Something in my gut says no, warming me inside like there's a fire starting to flare to life. I'm not going to give up like this. Even if I die—I'm not going to be starving when I do. I reach over and take the water and the protein bar, unwrapping it and taking a few quick bites before uncapping the water. Maybe I'll be able to plan a little better once I have food in me.

The lock clicks, and I almost spill water all over myself when my hand shakes. I didn't think he would come back this soon. What's going to happen now?

Then a dark head appears, but it isn't Enzo. It's the other one. Prince, I think his name was. Exactly what kind of name is that? I have no idea, but I'm not about to ask him how he got it.

"Hi," he offers, his voice deep and rich. He hasn't spoken much since I got here and never directly to me, at least not that I can remember. "How's it going?"

For a second, all I can do is gape at him in surprise. Is that an actual question?

He must take my reaction for what it is, and he laughs softly. "Of course. That's a stupid question."

What's his game? Why is he being nice to me? Is he the good cop, sent to warm me up, so I'll let my guard down and reveal these supposed secrets I'm carrying around in my head? I have to be careful.

"Thank you for asking, anyway," I offer, finishing off the

rest of the protein bar in a hurry like subconsciously I'm afraid he'll try to take it from me.

"Mind if I sit?" He gestures toward the bed, staying in place while he waits for an answer.

Now I know for sure something's up. Why else would he be this polite? Last night, he was looking at me like he couldn't stand the sight of me, and now he's asking permission to sit near me. Do I look like I just fell off the turnip truck or whatever the saying is?

"You're sort of running things around here," I point out as gently as I can. "You don't need to ask for my permission."

"There's something to be said for having manners, and I'm nothing if not polite." He takes a seat near the foot of the bed, careful to adjust his fancy suit pants before settling in.

"I'm sure this all seems confusing," he muses, and I hear the sympathy in his voice. The question is, is it sincere?

"Very," I agree, drawing my legs up tight against my body. I don't want any part of me coming into accidental contact with any part of him. He knocked me out—I can't forget that. In fact, the thought of it makes me lift a hand to the back of my head. It's swollen and stings when I touch it.

And he's always so polite? I wonder how he chooses to explain away this sort of thing.

He winces when he recognizes the gesture. "You'll have to forgive me for that."

"Do I, now?" I blurt out before thinking. Probably not a good idea to smart off to the man.

He takes it well enough, though, and chuckles softly. "It's up to you. In our line of work, you can never be too careful."

I'm still not sure how dangerous they thought I was going to be, unarmed and clueless, but I'm not going to argue.

"I really don't know anything. I wish you guys would listen to me."

"Like I said. We have to be careful."

I had to try, didn't I? I knew it wouldn't be enough to get through to him. He and his pal have a very definite idea of who I am. So what if they're completely wrong? There's no convincing them.

He eyes the empty wrapper sitting beside me. "That can't have been enough food. Do you want something else?"

My stomach growls like it heard him. Of course, a single protein bar isn't enough. But I'm also too upset to care much about eating, no matter how my stomach feels about it.

"I'm fine."

"Suit yourself. We can't have you wasting away to nothing." His gaze lands on my legs, eyes narrowing slightly as he studies them. "That would be a crime."

Goose bumps pebble my arms. "I wouldn't like it very much," I whisper, but he hears me anyway.

"No, I doubt you would." He's still staring at me, then creeps a little closer, his hand sliding over the duvet. "You know, you could make this easier on yourself."

I don't want him to know he's getting to me, but I can't sit here and allow him to get away with whatever he has in mind, either. I pull my legs even closer, my arms wrapped around them, my feet tucked in close.

"What are you so scared of?" he asks, chuckling. "I won't bite."

"I'm sure you don't." I watch him from over the tops of my knees. "But maybe I do. Ever think of that? Maybe I'm trying to keep you safe from me."

When he laughs, his face transforms into something a lot

more human. "You're funny. And you've got a backbone. You could scream and wail and be a general pain in the ass, but you haven't been. I've always had a weakness for women like you."

He reaches out, touching my calf, and I shuffle closer to the headboard. It's useless, though. This bed isn't very big, and he has extremely long arms.

"Please..." I'm shaking, and I'm sure he sees it, but that won't stop him.

"What? I'm not going to hurt you. But let's be honest. A girl like you with a body like this? Running around at night wearing a dress like that? Don't act like you're some innocent little thing." Suddenly, he grips my ankle, then jerks hard enough that he pulls my leg straight.

Oh my god, I'm going to be sick. Is this a game? Another test to see if I'll break down?

"Stop, please," I beg, my voice shaking.

"I'm just saying." He takes the other ankle, then pulls both of them until I slide farther down the bed. Now he's close to me, pawing at me. "If we both have to be here, why not have some fun?"

It's like trying to fight off an octopus—I push his hands away, but they only end up someplace else. On my breasts, my ass, my thighs, which are now bare thanks to the dress riding up. "Please, stop!"

"Prince!"

I barely register the sound of Enzo's roar and what it means before he grabs Prince by his suit jacket and hauls him off the bed, pulling him out of the room without saying another word. I'm weak with relief, ready to collapse. My heart's racing, blood pounding in my ears, and I want to go home. Why won't they let me go home?

The flash of realization breaks through my self-pity, and just in time.

He left the door open. I don't know where he took Prince, but he left the door open. This is it—my chance. I scramble off the bed before my brain can catch up with my body, peering up and down the hall and finding it empty. This could be a huge mistake, but I have to take it.

I run to the top of the stairs on my tiptoes, even holding my breath in case it helps. Where is he? Where did he take Prince? I'm not sure it matters because I'm getting closer to the living room, creeping down the stairs, and leaning over the railing to see if Enzo is nearby. I don't hear him. Maybe I'll finally get lucky, and he took him to a soundproof room or something. Unlikely, but who knows in a place like this? With people like this? I'm sure a soundproof room would come in handy.

The front door is right ahead once I reach the landing. I'm shaking so hard I can barely run in a straight line, but somehow, I manage it, my feet slapping against the hardwood, my arms outstretched. The door is locked, but it's only a plain deadbolt. All I have to do is reach it.

"Hey there."

No sooner do I hear his voice than the weight of his body slams me against the door I was only a second away from opening. And of course, that's not enough—he grabs the back of my neck and digs his fingers in, pushing me harder against the door until I'm afraid he might snap my bones.

"Now, what did you think you were doing?" he growls in my ear. "I know you weren't trying to get out of here, right? You wouldn't do something as pointless as trying to get away from me."

He leans in until I'm sure he's going to crush me. "Because, sweetheart, that would be a terrible mistake."

I have just enough room to pull in a deep breath, which I'm ready to let out in a scream because he's going to kill me. I know he is; this was the last straw. And when he clamps a hand over my mouth, I'm sure of it. No more letting me up for air at the last second like before.

"You don't want to scream," he continues before emitting a dark chuckle. "It'll only turn me on."

BEAST

8

ENZO

*T*his fucking girl. When is she going to learn to leave well enough alone?

"No. No. No," she screams from behind my hand like it will make any difference. Like I'm going to take pity because she doesn't want to be here. As if I want her here. As if I want to deal with any of this.

"You are way more trouble than you're worth." Especially since I can't seem to think straight with her body wiggling against mine, rubbing against me in all the best—or, depending on how I look at it, worst—possible places.

My hunger burns, desire unfolding low in my gut, the devil on my shoulder reminding me how easy it would be to take her here and now. There's nobody to stop me. Even Prince left, not wanting to face my wrath over the way he touched her.

"Keep it up," I growl in her ear. "The more you fight, the worse it will be when I shove my cock in your mouth. Or maybe I'll put it in this cute little ass you keep rubbing against it. Is that your way of telling me what you want?" Her enraged scream only makes me harder. I bet she'd be explosive in the right situation.

"Back to bed for you," I grunt, bitterly accepting the fact that I can't give in to anything as coarse and low-level as desire right now. Losers, weak assholes—they're the ones who lose sight of the end goal, too undisciplined to fight what they want here and now in favor of the bigger picture.

One of Renato De Luca's many lessons. It runs through my head as I lift her off her feet and carry her kicking and screaming back to the upstairs bedroom.

"This is probably my fault," I snarl. "I should have locked the door. I won't be making that mistake again." Her dismayed moan makes me laugh. She really thought she was being slick, like she could get away from me. All she's done is fuck herself over. I'll be doubly sure to secure her from now on.

I don't know whether it's a relief or a disappointment when I finally reach the bedroom and throw her onto the bed. She flips onto her back right away. Rage, hatred, and fear fight for control of her expressions as she scrambles back until she hits the headboard. Like she expects me to fuck her now. At least I know my intimidation tactics are working.

"Try some shit like that again," I warn, "and I won't be so nice. Do you doubt me?" When she's slow to respond, still breathless and almost weeping, I lean over her until she recoils in fear. "Answer me. Do you doubt a word I'm saying?"

"No." The word is feeble, but exactly what I need to hear.

"That's what I fucking thought. Don't let me hear you in here for the rest of the day if you know what's good for you." The slamming of the door almost drowns out her heartbroken wail. But not quite.

Let her be heartbroken, dammit. Some spoiled princess with probably no idea how the world actually works or the sort of sacrifices involved in our business. Pampered her entire life, expecting everything to turn out the way she wants it to simply because she said so. She'll be lucky if I don't take my frustration with her father out on her. Maybe I should remind her of that later; how easy it would be for me to vent my frustration on someone who shares Alvarez's blood.

Yet if Grandfather ever found out about that—and he would, I'm sure, he misses nothing—he'd have my balls for it. If I'm going to be head of the family one day, I have to learn to think strategically, not emotionally. I can almost hear his warning in my head as I pace the room that will be mine for the duration of this trip.

A trip that now seems like it will take longer than originally planned.

I have to do something, anything, to get rid of this ball of fire in my stomach, threatening to fry me from the inside out. Now that it's only the two of us in this house, the temptation to take all of this out on her is almost unbearable. That stupid motherfucker Alvarez. He thought he was being clever by leaving me hanging. Does he know what he's done? How easily I could make him regret his ignorance?

For lack of a better way of killing my erection, I locate the file Grandfather gave us for the purpose of brushing up on the Alvarez family and the Marielito. There it is, the line denoting the existence of a daughter. Elena. There's no more information on her aside from the fact that she's an only child.

Wouldn't a man without the benefit of sons be a bit more careful with his only child? Granted, in our world, women are generally treated as a means to an end. A subject to be bred for the gain or extension of power. Something to fuck or use as a means of solidifying family alliances through marriage. Yet without her, there can be no such alliance. He's losing some of the only capital he has. How can a man in his position not be smart enough to understand that?

I'd bet I could find a way to make her talk using the correct motivators. She thought the sensation of my switchblade pressed against her chest was scary? How would she feel about it if I offered to cut her a second slit between her thighs? Or maybe she wouldn't miss the presence of her nipples. Maybe I could offer to remove them for her.

Yet even now, storming around a bedroom that's only mine for the time being, part of me shrinks away from that idea. Not because it wouldn't give me pleasure. No, I have no doubt I would savor her screams, her promises, and apologies. The very thought of watching her unravel in front of me until I become the only god she knows revives my softening erection, heightening my hunger.

I shrink away from the idea because no one has ever reached that part of me before. The part of me Grandfather has struggled for so long, so unceasingly, to suppress or even silence.

"You have a darkness in you," he told me once, *"thanks in no small part to that bastard who fathered you."*

Never would he consider his daughter's blood to be the reason I'm like this. She was nothing less than a saint, an angel who deserved so much more than what life gave her.

Having met my father before ending his worthless life, I have no trouble believing that. I need to turn away from the creature my father turned me into, thanks to what he did to us. No matter how I crave the satisfaction, I can't sink that low.

Once I'm calm enough to control myself, I leave the room, walking slowly down the hall. I'm sure she can hear my footsteps, and the idea of her cowering on the bed while I pass sends a thrill through me. She would be such a nice way to pass the time.

I've never reacted this way to a woman, any woman. I've had more than my share, and they've all served the same purpose in roughly the same way. It's never difficult to attract them—the name De Luca is hardly unknown, and I suppose my father passed down decent genetics when it came to physical appearance. Money, power, looks? An aphrodisiac if there ever was one.

But it has always been the same. I meet one, she excites me for one reason or another, and by the time I've spurted out the last of what brewed in my balls, I can't wait to never see her again.

This Elena, on the other hand? I was ready the instant my body made contact with hers. It was that simple. Finding her at the door, pinning her against it, the friction her body made against mine. My cock sprang to life, and all of a sudden, it would be the simplest situation in the world. I have to take her, claim her, *own* her.

And it makes no sense. Hell, I got a better feel for her body last night when I carried her to the car. Yet while she was unconscious, she wasn't fighting. She was no longer the scrappy, feisty hellcat. Perhaps that's the missing link in all this. It isn't so much the girl but rather the fact of her not dropping to her knees at first sight, the way most women do once they know who they're looking at.

The thrill of something new for the first time in forever. That's what this is. Nothing more. Once I know how to brush off the situation, I can move past it. It's clear that I need to. I have to find a way past this if there's to be any hope of succeeding in what I've been tasked with. She will not get in the way of our plans. If anything, she might help move things along.

The beginnings of an idea brew in the back of my mind. I think I might know how to get through to her. It will just take another plan of attack. A new direction.

My phone rings, dragging me from my thoughts. It's an unknown number. "Yes?"

"Is this how your family does business? A man misses a meeting due to an emergency, and you take what belongs to him without so much as an acknowledgment of what you did?"

The hair along the back of my neck stands up. "Mr. Alvarez."

"Don't Mr. Alvarez me, boy," he warns in a deadly snarl. "You have something that belongs to me, and you're going to give it back."

∽

"What is this?"

I look down at the take-out containers, then back at her. She's sitting on the bed, pretending my presence doesn't worry her. Her back is ramrod straight, her chin lifted. The princess. It's quite a fitting nickname.

"You've never seen fast food before?" I place a box on the bed along with napkins. "A burger and fries."

She's not stupid enough to give me shit for assuming she eats meat or anything like that. And too hungry. Pride dissolves an instant before she flips the Styrofoam lid and picks up the burger, taking a huge bite.

"Did you ever consider the chances of me putting something in there?"

Her head snaps up, her cheeks bulging. Before she spits it out or chokes, I shake my head. "Kidding. I have no interest in poisoning you."

"What a relief," she mumbles before returning to her binge.

I sit at the other end of the bed and open my own container. "I'd like to have a conversation with you, Elena. A normal, one-on-one sort of talk. No screaming, no trying to run. Don't force me to regret taking this chance."

The wariness written all over her is a reminder of her intelligence. Granted, it failed when she attempted to flee, but she is, by and large, an intelligent girl. She had better hope that intelligence wins out now, or else everything that's passed until now has been child's play compared to what's ahead.

Because I cannot guarantee I'll be able to control myself if she begins shrieking and begging. I might forget what I came in here for.

"Go ahead," she grunts before taking hold of a few fries at once and biting into them.

I've never seen anyone eat like this before. I suppose protein bars aren't enough. Either that, or she doesn't see the point in manners at this point.

"After giving it a little thought, it became clear to me your father did not make you aware of what last night was about. Why I was at the warehouse." Her silence tells me I'm right, so I continue. "Prince and I were there for a first meeting with your father, in hopes of securing a deal between your family and mine. This would be a mutually beneficial arrangement, which we were assured your father was interested in pursuing. Yet he left me hanging. He never showed. He never contacted me."

She's no longer chewing, choosing to stare blankly at me instead. "Sorry? I'm not responsible for that."

"I realize that." She's determined to set my teeth on edge. I distract myself by biting into my burger, which is as delicious as she makes it seem. "The fact is, I brought you here on impulse, and now I need you to help me keep the situation from escalating."

"Me?" She blurts out a laugh. "If you want that, why have you treated me the way you have?"

"That can all be in the past," I offer. "We can start over with a clean slate. But that's up to you, too. I need you to behave yourself, and I need insight into how I can best manage your father."

"I know a surefire way to do it." She turns her full attention to me, leveling an even gaze my way. "Let me go home. I can't think of a better way to stir up goodwill."

She makes it sound so easy. I suppose I'd be able to do the same if I were in her shoes but I'm not, and therefore I have to do what must be done to protect myself and family.

BEAST

9
ALICIA

*E*verything was going fine until he showed up with dinner last night. I was starting to believe he was softening on me. But no, as soon as he showed up, back was the rough and menacing kidnapper. He even tied me up, saying I couldn't be trusted.

THERE I WAS, thinking I was going to get away. All I managed to do was make things worse. So much worse.

My hands are numb from my wrists being tied so tight. He wasn't gentle about it, but I wouldn't expect him to be as pissed as he was. I thought he was going to do worse than that.

It isn't worth thinking about what I thought. It only makes my heart pump faster as my stress reaction kicks in. I can't live in a perpetual state of fight-or-flight.

A few deep breaths help calm me down a little. It could be worse, right? At least I'm in a bed. At least this isn't some shithole.

And at least I know he won't let Prince touch me like he

tried yesterday. Of all things, that memory gives me the most comfort. Enzo was a complete madman when he burst in here and yanked his friend off me. If it wasn't for that, I'd be even more nervous at having my hands tied up, unable to defend myself.

While that memory eases some of my fear, it doesn't do much for my physical misery. Every muscle aches, and every joint is stiff and sore from having to lie here at all kinds of awkward angles. I never knew until now how much I need the use of my arms, even when I'm doing something as routine as sleeping. I couldn't roll over or adjust the blankets. I can't even brush the hair away from my face right now, no matter how hard I try to blow the few strands out of my eyes, and it's driving me crazy.

He can't leave me like this all day. Can he? The sun's been up for ages, a bright rectangle slowly inches its way from the floor to the wall opposite the window. I've heard movement elsewhere in the house. He has to know I'm going to need to pee, right? It's starting to go from a mild pressure to something a lot more demanding.

I'm sure he's trying to punish me a little more, the sick fuck. Making sure I'm good and sorry by the time he comes back to untie me. What did I do in a past life that led me to this? Because my karma must be seriously fucked.

"Untie me, please," I yell at the top of my lungs for Enzo, or anyone really. "I need to use the bathroom."

The door opens, and Enzo strolls in, looking me over before offering a wry little smirk. "You look good like this. Has anyone ever told you that?" he asks without acknowledging my request.

I don't want to answer, but I don't want to give him any

more reasons to be mad at me. "This is the first time I've ever been tied up like this."

I wish my heart wouldn't seize up like it does whenever I see him. It's too close to the way I used to feel when I was in middle school, and the boy I had a crush on would walk into homeroom on a Monday morning. Seeing him for the first time after the weekend always gave me that funny feeling in my chest. Is having a crush that close to the sensation of looking at the man who could blow your brains out at the drop of a hat?

His smile widens as he approaches the bed. "You mean I popped your cherry? Wow, this is a special honor."

"Please," I whisper when he doesn't make a move toward the ropes. "I really have to use the bathroom. Can you untie me?"

"Oh, so you think you're too good to lie in your piss?" He stands over me, scowling.

I realize he's serious. This isn't a joke to him, or maybe it is. Maybe he sees me as nothing more than a game to fiddle with.

"You want me to do it right here in the bed?" I whisper, horrified. Is there any end to the humiliation he wants to inflict?

He rolls his eyes before leaning over me to reach the headboard. "No, I don't expect you to do it right here. You think I feel like buying a new mattress?"

His touch on my wrists makes me flinch—but under that is something else. A shiver, and not a bad one, either. The sort of shiver that means anticipation.

He takes his time about it, though. His hands linger on me, his movements slow and deliberate. It makes me think back to something that flashed through my panicked, dismayed brain yesterday when he got me back in this room after catching me.

He likes this. I'd swear on anything that this is getting him off for some reason. Is he that broken?

Then again, I'm the one shivering in anticipation of his touch. Maybe I don't have any room to talk.

The blood starts flowing back to my hands as soon as the rope is gone, and I bite my lip against a pained groan. He's not sympathetic, but that comes as no surprise.

"Let's go. Do you think I have all day? You're the one who said you need to—"

I move before he finishes the thought, wincing as I get up from the bed. He clicks his tongue in mock sympathy before taking me by the arm, pulling me out into the hall, and leading me down to the bathroom.

"Don't make me fucking regret giving you privacy," he warns, shoving me into the room. "Abuse the privilege, and you'll have an audience from now on."

I nod shyly, fear and dread tying my tongue. He scowls at me again before closing the door. I know better than to think he'll move away from it.

But it's okay. At least he left me alone. I take care of business quickly, then wash my hands and face. I might as well since I don't know when I'll have the next opportunity. While doing that, I bounce up and down on the balls of my feet, stretching my legs. I don't know when I'll get the next chance to do that, either.

It would be stupid to think I could get away with using a weapon on him when I know he'll be watching everything I do. Besides, there isn't anything in sight that can be used to protect me. My sights land on the drawer, but there isn't enough time to search. The next time he allows me to use the bathroom, I'll look around. Maybe I'll be lucky enough to find something to hide somewhere for when the moment arises to try to get away again.

"Let's go. You don't need to run the water that long." He's right outside the door, his voice loud and clear enough that it's like he's pressed his mouth to the crack.

Shutting off the faucet, I dry my hands on the hand towel hanging next to the sink, then open the door to find him looking murderous.

"I'm sorry. I just wanted to freshen up a little."

"Who are you trying to impress?" he growls, pulling me down the hall again. It's been almost a full day, but he still hasn't cooled off any.

"You know, this could all go away, this whole misunderstanding." My insides clutch at the sight of the rope lying on the bed. I can't stand the thought of being tied up again. He seems like a man who knows how to negotiate when he has to —no, he's not working in a boardroom or anything like that, but I'm sure he's made deals before. This isn't some low-level flunky. Not in a house like this, dressed the way he is.

"Oh, could it?" Amusement flickers behind his otherwise empty eyes. Or maybe I only imagine them that way because he seems soulless?

"Sure. Let me go. Let me walk out of here. No harm done, I'm in one piece, I don't have any reason to go to the cops or anything. Besides, how could I prove it? I'm not interested in any of that. All I want is to go home. Please, I'm begging you." Because why not? What's pride at a time like this?

"So you think it's as easy as that?"

"Why does it have to be complicated?"

He stands in the doorway, his shoulders practically filling the frame. Not that I would be stupid enough to try to run past him at this point, not with him right here in my face, but it's obvious he wants to make sure I know he'll be on me again if I try anything.

"Don't tell me you're that naïve about how things go for people like us, Elena. I can only buy so much of the innocent act."

I should have told him the truth from the beginning. Now, if I tell him I'm not part of this family he thinks I'm related to, he'll take it as a lie. I can only imagine how much worse this would get if he thought I was lying to him all of a sudden. There's no way I can explain myself in a way that he'll understand—this is not an understanding person I'm dealing with.

"Besides," he continues, "I need you."

I gulp audibly. "You need me?"

"Don't get the wrong idea," he murmurs. The way his eyes rake over my body tells another story.

I wish my heart didn't skip a beat when he looks at me that way.

"You're leverage. I need to use you to get what my grandfather wants out of this deal. I have a meeting with your father in an hour."

Oh no. This isn't good. What's going to happen when the guy says I'm not his daughter? What happens to me, then? My pulse is alarmingly rapid, and my palms are all sweaty.

"Why would he want to make a deal with somebody who kidnapped his kid?" I ask.

He squints at me like I'm something he's never seen before. "Obviously, he'd want to be sure you didn't get hurt. He'll do anything to get you back. Most fathers would."

He's going to be very disappointed. And so am I when my head ends up on the chopping block.

"I don't know. I'd think letting me go would be, you know, a good faith gesture."

He smirks and even snorts a little. "Why so nervous? You don't think he wants you back?"

"Maybe I have a little more insight than you think. I'm just saying, I think it would go better if I was free before the meeting." It's wishful thinking, but what else do I have. The moment this Josef person shows up and sees I'm not who I've been pretending to be, Enzo will learn he has no leverage at all, and I'll end up with my brains all over the floor.

Then again, maybe not. Whoever this guy is, he might be willing to play along, right? He doesn't know who I am, but he'll know I was found with those drugs in my bag. He might want to keep me alive just in case there's something I know, something important. Or he might not want Enzo to know some random girl was given access to his product. It might look kind of unprofessional, now that I think about it. I'm sure Elena wasn't supposed to let me take her place.

And now I'm worried she'll end up getting in trouble. I really need to stop worrying about other people so much. My ass is on the line here, and I'm going to feel sorry for her? Has she even noticed that I'm missing or thought to look for me? But who am I kidding? Even if she had, what is she going to do? She's just a girl, involved with some very bad people. She told me as much.

I can't take the chance. I can't trust some mafia guy I've never met to protect me. So what am I going to do?

Only one thing comes to mind. And no matter how my body seems to enjoy being close to Enzo, this is not something I want to do. In fact, it's the last thing I want to do, but it might be enough to distract him.

So I do it before I can talk myself out of it, stepping up to him and placing my hands on his chest. "Are you sure there's nothing else you would rather use me for than leverage?" I whisper before taking the chance and brushing my lips against his—teasingly, lightly, scared out of my mind but trying to make it look like I want to be seductive. Will he go for it?

He takes me by the back of the neck, sinking his hand into my hair before deepening the kiss, consuming my mouth, and crushing my lips. I want to be revolted. I want to recoil in disgust. And part of me does; part of me is sickened and disgusted.

The rest of me? Another story. A sizzling current runs through my body like somebody plugged me into a socket, lighting me up inside. This shouldn't feel so good. I shouldn't be this hungry for him.

I shouldn't want him to put his hands on me.

He backs me up against the wall, holding me in place with his body the way he did when I tried to get away. But it's different this time. This time, I want him pressed against me, all over me. I can almost forget who he is and what this is about once his tongue slides into my mouth, sending a current directly to my clit.

It's probably not a bad thing when his hand tightens dangerously. I gasp in surprise, breaking the kiss, and open my eyes to find him glaring at me.

"Did I give you permission to touch me?" he whispers.

"I... I mean..." It would be great if I could think, but it seems all the blood left my brain in favor of rushing down to where I am now wet and aching.

For one breathless moment, he stares into my eyes, breathing heavily. Is it desire or rage, though? That's what I don't know. He kissed me as I had hoped he would. Now he's looking at me like he wants to kill me.

He opens his mouth to speak—then lets go of my neck and

steps back. "We have to get to the meeting. No fucking around and wasting time." His accent is thicker than usual now.

I can't believe I humiliated myself that way. All for nothing. Now he'll think I want him, and I don't like that one bit.

"And you're going to behave yourself, aren't you?"

When I don't answer right away, he lunges for me, this time curling his fingers around my jaw and pressing in hard enough that tears spring to my eyes and a pained whimper squeezes itself out of my throat.

"Aren't you?" he growls, baring his teeth in a snarl only an inch from my face.

Somehow, I manage to nod despite how strong his grip is.

He grunts. "I thought so. Otherwise, things won't go as smoothly as they have been until now."

This is smooth? I would hate to see what it would look like if things went poorly.

But something tells me I have no control over that. Because by the time this meeting is over, he'll know I'm not who he thinks I am.

And then? I might as well kiss my life goodbye.

BEAST

10

ENZO

We're fifteen minutes early for the meeting, scheduled to take place in one of the old hangars at an abandoned airfield a dozen miles or so from the townhouse. Prince has already studied the terrain, thanks to satellite images he combed once we were informed of the location.

"This place was a major hub in the middle of the last century," Prince explains as he drives the last few miles. "Very important to businesses like ours. Major shipments are coming in all the time."

"I suppose that makes it a natural choice for a meeting such as this," I muse since it seems he expects an answer.

"That, and the remote location."

I grunt my agreement, but really, I couldn't be less interested in the remote location at the moment, nor am I paying the sort of attention I ought to when it comes to watching for anything that seems out of the ordinary. Not that anything does—there's nothing around as far as the eye can see but tall grass swaying in the breeze.

But a lot of threats can hide in tall grass, just as much as they can in plain sight. Snakes, especially. Snakes like Alvarez. As the thought forms, I glance at the passenger side mirror and get a partial view of the Alvarez girl, daughter of the enemy, but soon to be the pawn to build this alliance my grandfather wants so desperately.

Her hands are bound in front of her, along with her ankles. She gave me no small amount of shit about that. "Remember what I said," I warn her. "Behave yourself if you hope to see your father."

She's staring daggers at the back of my head, and I wish it wouldn't amuse me so much. That feisty nature of hers. She can't hide from me. She's terrified, and I sincerely wish I didn't care why. I would think she'd be thrilled at the idea of being returned to the man. All she's done so far is complain that she wants to go home. If returning her is what it takes to get things moving with Josef, so be it. She's been nothing but a headache from the beginning, anyway.

And the fact that displeasure twists my guts at the thought of handing her over is confirmation that I need to get her away from me. She isn't my problem. I was stupid and reckless to take her in the first place, no matter how reasonable it seemed at the time. How necessary.

It's a hot, sticky day, and waves of heat rise from the pavement once we reach the old airport. Aside from the cracked concrete, nature has done its best to reclaim the area; weeds and small trees have haphazardly taken root. It's a bleak, depressing sight. So much ruin.

Prince is thinking along the same lines. "Can you imagine what this looked like back when it was thriving? The amount of money that passed through here. A river of it."

I can imagine armed men prowling the area, guarding shipments, and long, sleek cars going to and fro. Now there's little more than rusted siding, broken windows, and crumbling roofs as we begin passing the abandoned hangars.

Prince scans the numbers still visible above the hangar doors in hopes of locating the specific building we were instructed to report to, which he does after another minute of navigating what's left of the road. We hit a pothole, and the car lurches with us right along with it.

I notice the way he glances in the rearview mirror at Elena before muttering to me, "I don't like this. Do you feel it?"

I don't know what he's talking about, which makes me question myself. Prince's instincts are never wrong. I look around again, taking in the full scene, and it finally hits me. "Where is he?" There isn't so much as a car prowling the grounds, no men waiting outside the hangar we were instructed to meet at.

"Are you sure you have the right place?" I ask him—and immediately, I hear my grandfather speaking through me. He asked me a similar question not long ago, didn't he? And damned if it didn't irritate the hell out of me at the time.

He takes it roughly as well as I did. "You're more than welcome to do the recon from now on if it makes you feel any better."

He's right. Something is off about this. "You'd better hope your father didn't lure us into another little game," I warn Elena, who only turns her face toward the window. Does she know something? Was this all part of the plan? I want to shake the truth from her. Why can't I break this woman?

Is her father that determined to risk her? He was the one ranting and raving over my having possession of something that belongs to him. I would think he'd be pacing the tarmac, eager to get a look at his little girl. He never so much as referred to her by name during our conversation, speaking only of his property and how I had better return it undamaged.

There are only so many gestures of goodwill I'm prepared to offer.

We pull to a stop with ten minutes to spare. "I'll take a look around," Prince mutters as he puts the car in park. "Stay put." In another moment, I'm alone with her, and the tension in the air is thick enough to cut with a knife.

"Is this another one of your father's games?" I ask now that we're alone.

"Your guess is as good as mine," she whispers. "I don't know how to make you understand that I have nothing to do with any of this."

"You keep saying that, don't you?"

"I don't know why I bother. You refuse to believe me."

"That won't be your problem much longer, so long as your old man does what he promised."

I watch her in the mirror, hoping to catch a hint of the truth in her reaction. There's nothing about her to give me any deeper insight—she's either the world's greatest actress, or she's telling the truth. Is it possible she's nothing but an unwitting bystander in all of this?

It isn't my problem. I need to remember that. "I'm going to untie your ankles like I promised. But the second you decide to pull a bullshit move on me, that's it. You can forget any chance of seeing your father again."

"I understand."

I can barely hear her soft whisper. Not for the first time do I ask myself what sort of father Alvarez can be. She's afraid of seeing him, isn't she? Probably knows the shit he'll give her for getting herself captured. I have no doubt he'll grill her to make sure she didn't give away any family secrets. I'm sure I would do the same thing in his position. A small part of me considers insinuating she spilled her guts; if only to pay her back for the shit she's put me through.

The thought is enough to stir up a grim smile as I climb out of the car, slamming my door before opening hers. She tries to pretend she isn't afraid when I reach in and take hold of her, but I know better. She reeks of fear, a bitter, acrid odor. I've smelled it before on my enemies. I've even smelled it coming from myself once or twice.

"Something feels wrong about all of this," she whispers, staring over my shoulder as I loosen the knot. "Do you feel it?"

"Don't you start. Keep your mouth shut. Don't make me regret bringing you here." I'm quick to untie the rope around her ankles before stepping back, surveying the area. Prince is walking the perimeter of the hangar, his head swinging back and forth as he makes his way through the tall grass and the hidden obstacles. No doubt there's plenty of scrap metal and old tools, and God knows what else concealed by growth that's waist high in some areas.

I take a slow look around me, turning in a circle. The clock is ticking. Where is he?

It happens all at once. All I hear is the slap of her bare feet against the hot pavement before I turn around to find Elena running full tilt for the field only yards from where Prince parked. She drops the rope that was around her wrists only moments ago—the bitch untied it along the way.

"You fucking cunt," I growl, already hot on her tail. She's flying, running at a pace only desperation can inspire.

But I'm quicker. I have rage on my side.

What begins as a scream ends as a grunt when I take her down, forcing the air from her lungs once we hit the ground. I roll her over, pinning her with my body, but she still struggles.

"You still think you can get away?" I growl, snarling at her while she tries to twist her body from side to side, landing one ineffectual blow after another against my shoulders. "What's it going to take? What do I have to do?"

"Get off me!" She gasps, driving a knee into my ribs. Making her dress ride up higher than it already has, and instantly a deluge of dark fantasies flood my brain.

"You just can't resist, can you?" I growl, pinning her shoulders to the ground. She looks up at me with nothing but pure, seething hatred in her eyes, and all that does is make me more determined to make her regret this.

Before I can, her knee finds my balls—not a direct hit, not even all that hard, but enough to knock the wind out of me for a second. It's long enough for her to wiggle out from beneath me and fight her way to her feet. My arm shoots out, and I grab one of her ankles and bring her back down, pulling her to me while she cries out in frustration.

"So this is how you want it? You like it rough?" She moans out her dismay as I part her legs and yank her closer until my body is wedged between her thighs. "Maybe I'll send you back to your father with a few bruises?"

She fights like a wildcat, punching and clawing, slapping my hands away from every part of her I make contact with, giving me no choice but to take her by the wrists and slam them to the ground above her head. This brings me closer to her, and I don't know what takes hold of me. Rage, frustration, or maybe something even simpler than that. The way she turns me on the more she tries to fight. Whatever it is, it leaves me lowering my head and biting her neck, and I revel in the sharp gasp that comes from her when I do.

And in the way her hips jerk upward, grinding her pussy against my painfully erect cock.

It's a battle between fury and desire, the two fighting for dominance just like we are fighting in the grass. Now she's not fighting so much as she's groping—it isn't my cock convincing me of this, either. There's a difference between clawing when one's trying to inflict injury and raking one's nails over a man's back. Between trying to buck somebody off and fighting for contact.

That contact and the sight of my bite mark on her neck are an intoxicating mix. I'm as close to making a deadly mistake as a man can get, and those blazing eyes of hers are a challenge. I have to break her. I think she wants me to.

The crack of a gunshot changes the plan.

I get up on my knees, and Elena sits up with a gasp. "What—?" I cover her mouth with my hand, watching in horror as Prince collapses next to the car. Even at a distance, there's no missing the deep red stain spreading over the front of his shirt.

I shove Elena onto her back, still covering her mouth. A man dressed in black approaches the car and looks inside. Searching for something. For what? I don't know, nor do I have the chance to find out before pressing my body flat against Elena's and holding a finger to my lips. From where we are, I can no longer see what's happening by the hangar. I need to be able to hear, but all that fills my ears is the sound of her strangled whimpers and the blood rushing in my veins.

After what feels like an eternity, there's the revving of an engine, and moments later, the sound fades to nothing. When I take a chance and raise my head, I see what's left of a cloud of dust trailing behind the car fleeing the scene.

That's when I take her by the hand and haul her upright, running to reach Prince before it's too late.

If it isn't already.

BEAST

11

ALICIA

I've never been so tired in my whole life. I didn't know it was possible to be this tired and still be standing. Now that the worst is over, it's like my body and my brain have completely given up. Like I fought so hard to stay on my feet for so long that I have no choice but to shut down.

But Prince is stabilized. At least, I think he is. The bleeding seems to have slowed to nothing more than a slight oozing, and that's a hell of a lot better than the way it was at first.

As long as I live, I'll never forget the one-two punch of finding Prince lying flat on his back with his shirt soaked in blood—and realizing Enzo expected me to do something about it.

"We have to get him out of here," he barked, opening the back door of the car before dragging him inside. "And you have to help."

Me? I wished I had never told him I was studying anatomy and physiology. "I don't know what to do!" I screamed in horror and confusion. There was so much blood. It was one thing to know how much blood was in a person's body, but seeing it up close?

On top of that was hearing Prince's agonized groans as Enzo positioned him in the back seat. Every move was clearly torture. It wasn't like I cared one way or another whether the man died, but witnessing his agony was still shocking.

No more shocking than the gun Enzo pulled on me, pressing it to my temple. "Get in there and help him, or I blow your fucking head off!" He shoved me into the car and slammed the door before jumping behind the wheel and peeling away from the scene.

I had no idea what to do. And what was I supposed to do in a car, with no tools to help me? The best I could do as Enzo sped back to the townhouse was take off Prince's jacket, ball it up and press it tight against the bullet wound near his chest. "You'll be okay," I told him over and over, the words pouring out of me without conscious thought. Wasn't that what everybody said at times like this?

Once we got him to the townhouse, Enzo laid him out in one of the bedrooms after we carried him up the stairs together, with me taking his feet. Then I could tear away his shirt and get a good look at the damage.

"Fix it!" Enzo was crazy, his face red, his eyes wild as I scrambled around for towels, alcohol, anything I could think to use. I finally shouted at him to find these things for me—maybe not a great idea, shouting at a man like him in the state he was in, but it gave him something to do besides pacing the room like a wild animal.

As much as I absolutely didn't want to, I finally pulled the bullet from the wound using a pair of chopsticks I soaked in alcohol while Enzo held Prince still, a towel shoved in his mouth to bite down on and muffle his screams. Eventually, he passed out, which wasn't a bad thing since it meant I could concentrate a little better. "Don't worry, he's still alive," I told a frantic Enzo. "Just unconscious."

"You've got to fix this," he barked. "He's gonna bleed to death."

No shit. I didn't say that, of course, but considering I was the one who was supposed to be helping him, I had a pretty good idea of what could end up happening.

But that's over now, the wound sewn shut. I'm sure he'll have to be looked at by an actual doctor, but for now, he's stable. There's no bruising or swelling anywhere in his abdomen to tell me there's internal bleeding, so maybe he got lucky. It doesn't seem fair in a way, a man like him getting away with his life when I'm sure if the bullet had gone an inch off-course, it would have killed him. How many people has he murdered? I don't think I want to know.

But his survival means my survival, so I can't discount it.

"Is he going to live?" Enzo is still pacing, kicking aside one of Prince's shoes when it's in the way. The sound of it hitting the wall makes me flinch, and somehow that only seems to make him angrier. "Well?" he barks.

I brush back my sweaty hair with a bloodstained, shaking hand. "I think so. I'm sorry, I don't have any way of looking inside him."

"Don't get a smart-ass attitude with me. Does it seem like I'm in the mood for that?"

"I've done everything I can." I touch my fingers to Prince's throat to check his pulse. "It's strong and steady. I'm sure he'll be fine—if there's no infection. He really should get actual medical treatment."

"Let me worry about that."

"Fair enough." I look down at myself, realizing my condition for the first time. Hours have passed, but it might as well be a lifetime. I feel like a different person than I was before we left for that meeting that never happened. What went wrong? Would I have been shot if I hadn't run away? I'm too tired to actually ponder this—the question sort of floats around aimlessly in my head with so many others, like butterflies touching down for the briefest moment before fluttering away again.

What I can't avoid is what a mess I am. My dress is ruined; not like I would ever try to wear it again after this nightmare. I would rather burn it, honestly. There's blood on my arms, chest, and even my legs. So much blood. How can a person lose that much blood and live through it? The question makes me feel a little woozy, causing me to sway on my feet beside the bed.

"For fuck's sake." Before I know it, Enzo is by my side, catching me against him when I start to fall. "I don't need two of you in trouble."

"What are you doing?" I mumble, feeling confused. It doesn't help that he bends down and scoops me into his arms, lifting me off my feet. "What is this?"

"Relax already." He carries me to the bathroom and doesn't set me back on my feet until we're in front of the shower. "You're a mess. You need to get cleaned up."

Sure. If the room would stop rocking back and forth like we're on a ship in a storm, I might be able to do that. The simple act of reaching back to unzip my dress is too much.

"What are you doing?" I almost jump out of my skin when Enzo touches the zipper and begins lowering it. "No! Don't do that!" I twist around, trying to pull away, batting at his arms with both hands while my heart takes off like a scared rabbit, my panic response flaring to life again.

"Stop it! Calm down." But no matter how sharp he is with me, it only makes things worse. I crash against the vanity and almost fall to the floor when my knees buckle. He's going to hurt me. He's going to kill me.

"Get a hold of yourself." He pulls me to my feet and puts his arms around me, holding my arms at my sides. "You're freaking out for no reason. I'm trying to help you. Do you understand what I'm saying? Listen to me."

"Let me go!" I need to get away. I can't let him do this.

"Stop." A single word barked directly in my face. His arms are like steel, holding me in place no matter how I fight. "Breathe. Take a breath, as deep as you can."

Who is he to be acting like this? Like I'm freaking out for no reason? He's the reason I'm going through this. He's the reason I'm falling apart. What he made me do, what he's already done to me. Of course, I'm breaking. Anybody would.

"Breathe, dammit. One breath at a time. That's all you have to do now."

He's starting to get through to me, leaking into my fog of panic. And though a part of me doesn't want to follow his instructions, I don't have a choice. Either I breathe, or I pass out. And if I'm unconscious, he can do whatever he wants without me knowing about it.

Our eyes meet, and he pins me with his gaze. I can't do anything but what he's demanding. *Breathe in... out... in... out.* After a few of those, with Enzo following along, I'm not so close to shattering anymore.

"That's right," he murmurs, nodding slowly. His grip loosens, and he begins stroking my back with one free hand. "One after another." I do as he says, grateful now for his touch, for the way he seems to have everything under control. How can he be so calm after the fits he threw all night? How can he switch his temper on and off like that? I wish he'd give me a few pointers.

Finally, he unzips my dress all the way. It's pointless to fight and maybe childish. He's not trying to hurt me. He's trying to take care of me in a way I can't do for myself right now. I'm so far beyond the point of even the basics, too tired, too drained, and still haunted by Prince's screams and the blood that kept pumping from him for so much longer than it should have.

Once the dress is open, he spreads the back with both hands, then slides it over my shoulders and down my arms. He unhooks my strapless bra and lets it fall between us. He says nothing, staring for a moment at my boobs before letting go of me so the dress can pool at my ankles. Goose bumps pebble my skin, and I expect him to do more than stand still while I drop my panties, but he hardly glances down.

I have to remind myself to breathe the way I did before. It isn't panic threatening to steal my breath this time. It's being naked in this man's presence.

I tense up when he reaches for me again, sucking in a scared, sharp breath. "Relax," he murmurs, pulling me closer, even brushing his lips against my neck. "You're going to be fine. Everything is going to be fine."

Why is he doing this? Being so gentle and even sweet? And when he touches his lips to my skin, all I want is to lean against him and beg for more. This is the last man I need to beg for anything, but especially this. He holds my life in his hands, and I'm craving his touch. It's absolutely twisted.

But right now, it's what I need. And somehow, he knows that.

"We're going to get you washed up now."

I nod, exhausted, glad to let somebody else deal with logistics for a moment. I can shut my brain off while Enzo turns on the shower. I step into the stall, immediately assaulted by the sting of hot water against my skin. But it feels good.

Leaning against the tiled wall, I close my eyes, letting the water run over my body. Maybe it can wash away the memories, too. A moment later, the door to the stall opens, and I go rigid all over again when a shirtless Enzo reaches into the shower to pour body wash over a washcloth.

"Just relax," he murmurs, and something about his low growl comforts me. Like every word he says picks at the knot of tension between my shoulder blades and in my stomach, loosening them a fraction at a time. "Turn around. Let me get your back."

I'm too relieved at being taken care of to insist on washing myself. I turn away from him so he can begin to slide the soapy cloth over my neck and then across my shoulders and down. He works slowly, but there's nothing inherently sexual about his touch.

That doesn't stop me from having to stifle my sighs, worried he'll take them the wrong way. Really what I'm more worried about is him taking them the right way, interpreting my reaction for what it is. I can't let him know what he does to me. I might be half dead from exhaustion, but I know that much.

He doesn't bother telling me to turn around, using his hands to turn me in place. I close my eyes and tilt my head back so the water runs over my hair while he washes away the dried blood that seeped through my dress. Every touch is like magic, unwinding me a little more, so by the time he decides I'm clean enough, I feel loose and content.

He even wraps me in a big, fluffy towel before backing away so I can step out of the stall. He towels off his wet chest and arms quickly, and I can't help but sneak a few peeks at his ridiculously chiseled shoulders, biceps, and abs. He's the product of discipline, obviously, with the body of someone who drives himself hard and unmercifully. He's just as hard on himself as he is on others.

"Feeling better?" he asks when he catches me watching him.

I have to avert my gaze, nodding while toweling off my hair. At least the towel hides my face, now flushing thanks to embarrassment. "Yes, thank you."

"Good. Come on." I have no choice but to follow him out of the steamy room, but instead of leading me back to the room I've stayed in since I got here, he takes me farther down the hall. I follow slowly, with hesitation. Does he know what he's doing? Did he forget to drop me off?

He opens the door, and I find myself in a large, sunny room with a king-size bed. Now my heart is racing all over again. Is this what he was cleaning me up for? No matter how much my body wants him, this can't be right. How naïve am I, thinking he only did that to be nice? When am I going to learn?

He turns to me, then frowns as his gaze moves over my face. "What? What's the problem now?" I'm too afraid to talk, but the direction my gaze moves in—the large bed with its piles of pillows and what looks like satin sheets—answers his question. "I brought you in here to get dressed. That's all. Calm down." He keeps telling me to do that, doesn't he? I doubt I could make him understand how impossible it is to be calm around him. Not when he's so unpredictable, and he's been so damn cruel and violent.

Instead, I settle for sitting on the edge of the bed, shaking a little while he opens the door to a vast closet that looks more like the interior of an upscale men's store. Black walls, dark wood shelving, and a table in the center holding watches and cuff links that gleam in the light from tastefully recessed fixtures. There's an entire wall of suits, and the one opposite holds dress shirts, along with a rack of ties. The man has good taste. I wonder what it would be like to have a closet like this, full of expensive clothes and shoes and jewelry.

I wonder what it would be like to live such a dishonest life that I'd be able to afford such things. Nobody makes this kind of money legally, and it isn't like I have any illusions about this man. He's a criminal, plain and simple. A criminal with an extraordinary closet.

He pulls a shirt from inside and buttons it up, barely glancing my way in passing. "Don't just sit there. This isn't an invitation to stick around. Put on some clothes."

To my surprise, he leaves me alone, shaking a little, wondering if this means he trusts me a little more now.

And I'm afraid of what that means and what might happen next.

BEAST

12

ENZO

*P*rince is still unconscious, though he's breathing and no longer has that gray pallor to his face. "I'm going to make sure he pays for this," I promise in a low voice, shaking with rage. "I promise you that."

The fucking bastard. It's obvious he never had any intention of going into this potential deal in good faith. He's done nothing but jerk me along from the beginning—all his posturing and bitching over the phone was an act, clearly. He cares nothing about the girl I'm holding, not if he was ready to pull a stunt like that. I might as well be fighting smoke, trying desperately to take hold of it and bend it to my will. All it does is slip away.

I've never shrunk back from what needs to be done, but his actions surprise even me. How do I win against a man with no principles whatsoever?

The question weighs heavily on my mind as I descend to the living room and sink onto the sofa. I could sleep for days if only my mind would allow it. I can't shut off my thoughts; questions and accusations drift to the surface.

I hear her before I see her approaching the top of the stairs. "I'm sorry. I hope you don't mind that I chose this."

Mind? The sight of her in one of my white dress shirts might be one of the sexiest things I've ever seen. I have to get a hold of myself before my jaw drops. Even when I manage to control my reaction, I can't help but stare at her as she descends the stairs. Slowly, tentatively, chewing her bottom lip the entire time. All that does is make my mouth go dry. She is determined to tempt me at every turn.

"Not at all," I murmur, barely holding on to myself. Now that I've seen her body and touched her, the temptation is more impossible than ever to ignore. And I can't forget how she burst into flames under me out there before the gun went off and everything went to hell with Prince. She was close to giving in, I know it. I'm sure that's the last reaction she expected to have, but there was no denying it. Given another few moments, I would have been inside her.

I would never consider Prince's shooting a good thing, but the timing might have been on our side the longer I think about it.

"Please, have a seat." I gesture toward the other end of the sofa. "We need to have a talk."

She may as well be walking to the electric chair. Folding her arms over her middle, she takes one slow step at a time. "I did the best I could with Prince," she whispers. "I really did."

"That's not what this is about." It's almost funny that she thinks it is. She's lost sight of the big picture, and I have no problem reminding her.

"Oh." She lowers herself onto the sofa, sitting up straight with her hands folded in her lap. The very picture of a good girl. If she knows what's good for her, that good-girl attitude will follow her into our conversation. She wants to please me. It's in her best interest.

"Here's how this is going to go." I angle my body toward hers and read the fear in her eyes. It was always there, but now it's stronger. More potent. "You are going to be honest with me. You are going to answer my questions clearly, immediately, and you will not tell me any lies."

I reach into my pocket, closing my fingers around the switchblade she's already familiar with. She sucks in a sharp gasp at the sight of it. "Or else, I have to be honest with you, I can't promise I'll be able to control myself."

As it is, the sight of her fear is too intoxicating. I want to teach her the true meaning of fear. I need to. It's the only way I'll ever find any peace.

"What if you ask me something, and I don't know the answer?"

"I think you will. I think if you want to live through this, you're going to have the answers I want. I think you're suddenly going to remember a lot of things you only thought you'd forgotten. But these won't be stories you're telling me. They'll be the truth, the entire truth." I open the knife and study my nails before I begin cleaning them with the edge of the blade. "Indicate your understanding of what I just said."

Every silent second that passes between us is like the turning of a knob, ratcheting up my tension. Making it more likely I'll lose myself in the process of punishing her.

Finally, she emits a whimper. "I don't know what you want, but I'll do my best."

"Your best isn't good enough. You're going to give me what I want. No more of these games, Elena, or else what nearly happened to us earlier will become a reality—for you, not for me. I have no intention of losing my life today."

And oh, she shudders, and it's a beautiful thing. Perhaps one day, I'll have the opportunity to look back over the way I react to her and analyze it. It isn't that I'm the type of man who's ever shrunk back from inflicting pain, but it's never pleased me nearly as much as it pleases me to watch her suffer.

"I'm going to start with an easy question." I look up from my nails to find her staring at the knife, unblinking. "Why would your father send a hitman to kill us before he had ever verified whether you were safe?"

"I swear, I don't know. I had no idea that was going to happen!"

"That's not what I asked you." I wave the knife slightly, and she gulps. "I asked why he would send a sniper before he had even set eyes on you. It's obvious he wasn't there and had no intention of arriving. A single sniper, that's all."

"I'm telling you." Her voice is barely a whisper like her throat is too tight for more than that. "I don't know. This is all a mystery to me, and I know you don't believe that, but it's the truth."

"We can agree on that much. I don't believe you."

"But it's the truth. I don't know any other way to put it. I'm telling you the truth. I don't know what he's thinking. I don't know why he would do that. I don't know anything about the way he does business."

The thing is, I believe that. It wouldn't be the first time a man in his position ignored a daughter. "Do you have any male relatives your father plans on handing the family business down to once he's gone?" It's a trick question. I already know the answer, which is no. There was no mention of another male relative in the file my grandfather provided.

"No?"

Right answer, but not exactly delivered in a reassuring way. "Are you guessing?"

"No." She's firmer now.

"So there is no male relative marked as the heir. This tells me you are the only option."

Her brows draw together as if she's in pain. "No."

"You mean to tell me your father has no contingency plan in place? I think we both know that's impossible. It just doesn't happen that way." I slide over, and she lets out a strangled little whimper. "So I know you're lying. If there is no male relative—and I know there isn't, good on you for telling me the truth about that—it means you are a valuable asset."

She falls back slightly when I lean in, inhaling the scent of the soap I used to wash her earlier. "Yet he allowed a sniper to open fire on one of us without first confirming your safety. You tell me. In what world does that make any sense?" Before she can open her mouth and spew out another lie, I begin running the tip of the blade up her bare calf. She freezes solid and with good reason. The slightest bit of pressure, and I'll break the skin. She's a fool, but she's not that stupid.

"Now I know your father doesn't care whether you get hurt or not," I muse, watching as I trace a line up her calf and leave a faint pink stripe behind. "So there's nothing stopping me from breaking the skin."

"Please, don't."

"There's nothing stopping me." I glance up and meet her terror-filled gaze. "I'm sure you know better than to think you can."

"I don't see why you're punishing me for what he did. Obviously, I haven't been in contact with him. I don't know what he's thinking or why he would do what he did. And I busted my ass to save Prince's life, by the way. Doesn't that earn me any credibility here?"

I have to give her credit. Her voice is trembling almost as hard as her body, but she managed to get that out. She's not entirely wrong, either.

But I need to understand the man's mind. "Is he that ruthless? That he would sacrifice his only child the way he did?"

"Maybe he thought he would take a chance? You would have to ask him."

I pause when I reach her knee—then keep going. She sucks in another gasp through her clenched teeth, and her chin quivers. "Was that the reason you ran? Because you knew what was coming? Don't lie to me."

"I-I only wanted to get away. I didn't plan it. I just wanted to run."

"Because you knew someone would come out firing at us."

"That's not true," she says. I press a little harder, causing her to wince. "I swear!"

"I don't believe you," I growl, frustration mounting. "Why do you keep lying to me?" With my free hand, I begin unbuttoning the shirt from the bottom up, and each button bares more skin for me to run my blade over. The muscles jump and twitch in her abdomen.

"I'm not." Tears start to roll down her cheeks, dripping from her quivering chin. It's a true sight to see. "I'm not lying. Stop saying that."

"I'm sorry. Did you just tell me what to do?" I pop another button, another, then spread the shirt open to bare her tits. They're nice tits, even better than I imagined, full and heavy with light pink nipples. "It would be a shame to slice up tits this nice."

She releases a shuddery breath. "Oh, god, please."

"This is entirely up to you."

"I don't know what you want from me!" She's breathing so fast that I wouldn't be surprised if she hyperventilates. Her eyes are glued to the blade, and a high-pitched whine works its way out of her. "Please, don't do this."

I barely hear her. Not when my entire awareness is focused solely on the way her flesh reacts to the steel threatening to pierce it. I can't take my eyes from it, her soft, supple breast and the light gleaming from the knife.

"What am I supposed to do about this?" I look up into her eyes, pleased to find them wide and brimming with fear. "How do we handle this?"

"I don't know. Please, I don't know. Why are you doing this to me? I've never hurt you. I've never hurt anyone!"

"Now you're boring me." Finally, I reach for her nipple.

"Oh, my god," she whispers.

"You don't need both of these, do you?"

She flinches away from the tip of the blade, now circling her nipple, her high-pitched whining fading to the background of my awareness in favor of the blood rushing in my ears. The power of holding her in my hands like this, knowing I could change the course of her life with a single flick of the blade. She would never fucking forget me, would she? And every time she looked down at herself, saw herself in a mirror or watched a man's expression turn to one of horror at her mangled flesh, she would remember how she screwed with me. Lied to me, kept me dangling like I'm some sort of fucking joke.

"Set up another meeting!"

I pause, looking up at her. "Excuse me?"

"Ask for another meeting. Tell him…" Her eyes dart around. "Tell him you're not happy about what he did, and now you want him to make it right by meeting for real, face-to-face. Tell him it's his last chance or something like that."

"You believe he would respond positively to an ultimatum?" I'm close to sitting back, her response having caught me off guard.

"Do you have any other options?" When I lift an eyebrow, she recoils. "I'm just saying."

"And this wouldn't be an attempt at getting me killed, would it?" I add the slightest pressure and marvel at the speck of blood that seeps against the silver blade.

"No! Oh, please, don't hurt me!" She moans, and it's the sweetest sound.

"Because it sounds a lot like you're suggesting I give it another try since your father wasn't successful in killing me the first time around."

"No, no, that's not it. I swear. Please, believe me." She hangs her head and weeps—and the sound grows louder, almost gusty, once I pull the blade away. Instantly, she closes the shirt and curls into a ball, arms around her knees, her chin tucked close to her chest.

I can't bring myself to take pleasure when there are too many questions fighting for control in my tired brain. Is this all an act? Is she plotting behind those tears?

If I'm not careful, this supposedly simple mission is going to drive me out of my head.

BEAST

13

ALICIA

$\mathcal{A}$t least I'm not tied up anymore.
It's amazing how something as small as that can end up meaning so much. Is this how Stockholm Syndrome develops? Things are so bad at first that when they get incrementally better, the person being held captive is so grateful they end up becoming attached to the person who took them?

That must be what's going on now, and all I can think is that I have to stop it. I can't let myself start thinking about him as anything more than a monster. And he wonders why I can't relax around him? Then he goes and pulls some psychotic nightmarish shit like he did earlier.

I guess it's better that I don't understand. If I did, it would mean I was no better than him.

He's left me alone since then and hasn't demanded I go back to my room, but I returned there anyway if only to be away from him. He's too unpredictable. I can hardly breathe when we're in the same room; his energy is so intense, so suffocating. How am I supposed to live in the same house with this man when I don't know if he's going to be sweet or pull a knife on me? We can't even have a conversation without things getting violent.

Still, I can only hide in the bedroom for so long. Especially when my stomach won't stop growling. I haven't been given free access to the house or anything like that, but he didn't tell me anything was off-limits either. Should I take a chance and see if I'm allowed to eat? Sheesh, how dehumanizing is this whole situation?

Eventually, hunger wins out over apprehension, and I have no choice but to tiptoe out of the room and down the stairs, listening hard for any sounds coming from elsewhere in the house. It's quiet, but that doesn't give me any comfort. If anything, now I'm wondering what's coming next. Is he planning something? Waiting like a snake in the grass, looking for any opportunity to strike? I find myself peering over my shoulder left and right at every turn I make in the house. When I reach the kitchen, I'm a nervous ball of energy.

At least it's empty—but not empty of food. I'm not trying to be picky, and I'm not trying to take a lot of time, which is why I grab for the protein bars in the first cabinet I open. At least I know they're good from eating them before. I grab two, then snatch a bottle of water from the fridge. I'm probably better off dashing back upstairs where I can be alone. As boring as it is up there, it's better than running the risk of being discovered wandering around down here.

I'm halfway to the stairs when I hear his heavy footfalls coming down the hall. It's amazing the panic that blooms in my chest when I hear his footsteps, the terror that races through me while I look around for someplace to hide. If he can't see me, he can't use me as a way of venting his anger. That's all that matters right now, making sure he doesn't use me.

But there's nowhere to hide, and now he's coming down the stairs. I'm frantic, but I finally settle on taking a seat at the kitchen table for lack of anywhere else to go. I'm just going to sit here and behave myself. I'm sure he walked past the open bedroom door anyway, so he has to know I'm around somewhere. Maybe if he finds me sitting here like this instead of testing the lock on the front door, it will earn me some trust.

By the time he reaches the living room and looks through to where I'm sitting, I've already unwrapped one of the protein bars and am munching quietly. Our gazes meet, but he's the first to look away. It wasn't fast enough to hide his scowl, though. I guess I shouldn't have taken it upon myself to sneak down here. Then again, he hasn't said anything, so who knows? Trying to figure out what he's thinking is a total waste of time. I can't predict him.

From the corner of my eye, I watch him cross the room, heading to the bar cart set up between the living room and kitchen. He doesn't say a word or even glance my way, pouring himself a drink that he quickly throws back in one quick, smooth motion. How does he do that? I'd be gasping and choking right now if I even tried.

Instead of setting the glass down, he only refills it, then turns his back to me in favor of flopping down on the sofa and turning on the TV. Soon, the ear-splitting sounds of an action movie drown out the thudding of my heart. It's not necessarily a bad thing, especially if it keeps him occupied.

He's got to be just as tired as I am now. I doubt he's gotten any sleep after Prince's close call. I lean back in my chair a little, so I can see him, sitting there with his drink in his hand, resting on his knee. He's staring at the TV, but I get the feeling he's not actually seeing anything in front of him.

He's practically chugging whiskey, and after everything he

put me through today, I can't help but think he's preparing for something. Psyching himself up. Am I being overly paranoid, or is this my intuition telling me to get ready in case something bad happens?

He didn't even think to get mad at me for being in the kitchen, where there are knives and other potential weapons. Granted, I didn't think about stealing any of them, which kind of makes me wonder about myself. I'll chalk it up to fatigue.

Now it's too late to arm myself, of course. He'll see if I get up and grab a knife. I might as well use that knife to slit my own throat since that's probably what he'd end up doing with it anyway.

The energy in the air is enough to make my skin crawl. I just wish I knew what he was thinking. Why is he sitting there, sipping the whiskey he almost filled the entire glass with? What's he planning? He's got to be planning something.

Dammit, I have to get out of here. Even if he isn't planning something, he's going to end up getting drunk if he isn't already. What happens if he decides to hurt me for real? It's bad enough he is already frustrated since things don't seem to be going his way. I can't sit here and let this happen. My skin's crawling, my palms are sweating, and I'm about to scream from the tension.

When his head starts to nod, I think I've found my way out.

But that's only part of the puzzle. Sure, if he passes out, it leaves me free to escape. But I can't just walk out of here wearing nothing but a dress shirt and panties, can I? What's the alternative? Going upstairs, hoping to find a pair of pants with a drawstring in that enormous closet? Because anything of his will drop right off me otherwise.

Then again, the shirt falls halfway down my thighs—it's not much shorter than the dress I was wearing when I got here. And if it means getting away, I can stand the embarrassment of being discovered while half-naked and barefoot. So long as I'm discovered. So long as it means getting away.

My pulse is racing, and I can barely hold myself still as nervous energy begins to make my limbs shake. I still have to hold back, waiting to see if he'll finally lose consciousness. I doubt he would go to bed without forcing me to do the same, so he has to fall asleep where he is.

Which means I'll have to sneak past him and open the door quietly enough that he won't be roused. Well, he might have done me a favor with his choice of entertainment since the gunfire and explosions on the TV will probably drown out the sound of the door swinging open. I only hope the action doesn't die off at the wrong moment. Wouldn't that just be my luck? No. I can't even afford to think that way. This is going to be fine. Everything is going to turn out just the way I need it to. I need to think that way.

The only other thing I need is my bag, which is still sitting on the floor on the other side of the sofa. He hasn't touched it since he left it there after finding the drugs inside. I could sneak past him to get it, right? I have to. There's no other choice.

Come on, come on, go to sleep. My body is a live wire, every ounce of my attention focused on whether he's asleep or awake. Whether he's pretending or not. What if he's faking it to see what I'll do? What if this is all a way of testing me?

I can't afford to think that way. I can't talk myself out of this, no matter how scary it is. I can't let him wear me down until I stop trying to save myself. Talk about Stockholm Syndrome. I'm not going to let it happen.

Finally, his chin touches his chest. I can hardly breathe, I'm so scared. *You can do this. One step at a time.* I can't afford to let fear get in the way, so I make a mistake.

Once a few minutes pass, and it seems like he might legitimately be asleep, I rise from the chair as quietly as possible and begin tiptoeing into the living room. There's still plenty of action going on in the movie, so I use it to my advantage, slipping past him before slowly bending down to reach for my bag on the other side of the sofa. I never take my eyes off him, noting the way his chest rises and falls slowly, evenly. He might even be snoring a little, but I can't quite tell over the sound of a brutal fight going on on the screen behind me.

Finally, I pick up the bag and begin backing away, still watching him for even the slightest twitch. He's out cold; what little is left of his second drink sitting on the coffee table. Maybe that's all it took to finally calm down enough that the action and tension of the past couple of days have caught up to him.

I reach out behind me with one hand, feeling around for the door. My fingertips touch the wood, and I start creeping closer to the knob, which I finally close my fingers around. Not so much as a twitch from him yet. Oh, god, this could be it. I could escape.

But not quite yet. I have to finally pry my eyes away from him to find the lock. I turn it slowly, holding my breath, my gaze darting back and forth between it and the man I'm seconds away from escaping. So close.

Finally, with the lock disengaged, I have to go for it. I turn the knob and ease the door open just far enough to slide through.

And that's all it takes. I'm free. Standing on the front step, fresh air hits my face, stirring the shirt around my thighs. For one brief, beautiful moment, I'm invincible. Nothing can touch me. I did the thing that scared me the most, and I lived through it.

What a shame my feet leave the step a split second later. A scream rips from my throat but is cut off by a hand clamping over my mouth. "Fucking bitch," Enzo snarls, carrying me back into the house while I kick my feet as an attack, even though it doesn't help. Right now, nothing will help.

Disappointment rushes through me. I was so close. Now he's going to kill me for sure. He hauls me upstairs to the bedroom—each step up the stairs brings me closer to what has to be certain death. I claw and scratch at his hands and arms, but it does me no good. I might as well not fight him at all. As soon as we enter the room, he tosses me onto the bed in a screaming heap.

"I'm sorry! Please, don't hurt me!" I know it's no use, that I might as well be talking to myself, but it pours out of me all at once.

He doesn't even acknowledge that I'm speaking, instead tearing the shirt open right down the middle. For one horrifying moment, I know this is it. He's not just going to kill me; he's going to rape me first. When he starts stripping the shirt from me, I fight with all I have, but all he does is grab my wrists and wrap the shirt around them before using it to tie me to the headboard.

"Please, please! I just want to go home! That's all, just let me go!" I sob, twisting and squirming with my arms over my head. It's no use. He's tied me tight, and every tug only makes the knot that much more impossible to loosen.

Instead of acknowledging a word I'm screaming, he climbs onto the bed, straddling me before bending down until his face fills my field of vision. The stench of whiskey is thick enough to choke me. "You can never leave well enough alone, can you?" he demands. His eyes, god, they're so dark and empty. *Evil.*

"I just want to go home. Why don't you get that?" I whimper, praying maybe he can see how truthful I'm being.

"And if your father would act like a man and come to the table to do business, you could go home." My father again. It's too late now to tell him that man is not my father. I'm dead, plain and simple. It seems like no matter what I do, I'm going to end up losing my life. I can't bring myself to pull the trigger —no pun intended. Besides, I don't even know if he would believe me if I finally confessed.

"But that's fine," he continues, pressing his body against mine. And despite the fear rippling through me, it feels good, which only throws my brain into worse confusion than before. I don't know if I'm writhing and bucking my hips in a vain attempt to throw him off me or because I want more of me touching more of him. Am I really this far gone?

His fingers trail along my jaw, then my throat. He touches me like I'm a rare jewel, like I'm fragile, and I tense up in preparation for what I know is coming. We've played this game before, and even though I'm terrified, heat blooms in my core, too. It's like my body is determined to betray me.

Strange enough, he doesn't grab my throat. Instead, his fingers trail down my chest, between my breasts, and over my rapidly beating heart. I look up at him, wondering where this is going, and all I see is the face of a man determined to get revenge.

We stare at one another before he breaks the silence. "I'll use you to make it happen," he announces in a deceptively soft voice. "And when I do, he's going to regret ever fucking with what's mine."

BEAST

14

ENZO

"Remember what I told you." It's difficult to rein in my amusement at the way she struggles. "The more you fight, the more I like it."

"You're fucking sick," she spits out. Little does she know how that turns me on, as well. The white-hot hatred is now rolling off her in waves, threatening to drown both of us in its depths.

"Do you think that comes as any surprise to me? I'm well aware of my faults and weaknesses. You are not telling me anything I haven't already told myself."

"I'm glad you're enjoying this."

"If that makes you glad, you'll be so much happier once I get started in earnest."

"And what does that mean?"

"Do us both a favor, and don't play dumb. You've made questionable decisions, I'll grant you, but I doubt you're stupid. You know exactly what I mean."

Where to begin? So many options. I'm a boy in front of a

Christmas tree, gifts galore spread out as far as the eye can see. The only question is, which do I unwrap first?

"What are you doing?" She makes a weak attempt at bucking me off when I kneel on the bed and run a hand up her bare leg.

"What do you think? I'm having a little fun. I might as well, right? I'm certainly not getting what I need from you in any other way."

She flinches when my hand creeps higher and higher over her bare thigh. "So soft," I murmur, genuinely impressed. "So nice to touch. Do you really want to deny me the opportunity to touch you?"

Gritting her teeth, her response is as I suspected. "Yes, that's exactly what I want."

"That's a shame. But you aren't going to get what you want. I would tell you I'm sorry, but that would be a lie." I dig my fingers in up high, close to her hip, and her strangled gasp only makes me grip her harder. The need to mark her is feral. "You and I, we haven't had nearly as much fun as we could. I plan to rectify that."

"And what does that mean?" she whispers, struggling fruitlessly against the shirt holding her wrists immobile over her head.

"See this?" Reaching into my back pocket, I pull out my phone. "Maybe it's time I remind your father what's at stake."

Horror is the only word to describe what washes over her face, almost contorting it into something unrecognizable. "You wouldn't do that!"

"Have you forgotten who you're talking to? Of course, I would. Gladly, since the son of a bitch is playing one big game of chicken. Wanting to see which of us will blink first. We'll see how much blinking he's willing to do once he gets a look at his baby girl tied to my bed." She starts twisting, screaming out her rage and indignation. All I can do is laugh while inside a storm has begun to rage.

Dammit, she is tempting. Such spirit, too. Practically begging me to break that spirit, to grind her into nothing but a pliant, malleable thing I can use for my pleasure, at my will.

But no, on second thought. I like her better this way. Trying to kick me, snarling, working herself into a sweat with every ineffectual swing of her leg, every time she tries to drive a knee into some part of me or another.

"All you're doing is exhausting yourself," I murmur, clicking my tongue in mock concern. "You have to know nothing is going to change, no matter how you fight. So why bother?"

"You're disgusting, and foul, and a horrible human."

"Once again, tell me something I don't already know."

She wails in dismay when I fondle her tits, judging their size, holding up my phone with my other hand in a silent threat. She surprises me by gritting her teeth, an animal growl stirring in her chest as she begins tugging the shirt in earnest. She fights so hard, in fact, the knot I tied at the headboard begins to loosen.

"Settle down," I warn, leaning over her to fix the problem.

All that does is create another problem, namely the way she fights and wiggles and rubs herself against me in her struggle. I close my eyes and force a shaky breath into my lungs. I have her right where I want her, utterly in my control. It would take nothing to finally claim her and, perhaps if I'm lucky, cleanse her from my system. That might be what I need to calm the storm raging just beneath the surface.

Raging like the erection I now have, thanks to the way she bucks and writhes beneath me.

"Oh, yes," I murmur, breathing heavier. "Keep going. Just like that. All you're doing is making me harder."

Her features fill with utter disgust. "Fuck you."

"I would much rather fuck you, Elena." Once I'm convinced she's secure, I back away slightly but remain on the bed. "Why didn't your father regret letting me keep you under my control? Knowing he could have spared you this if only he had played fair?"

She turns her face away from me, and anger starts to seep into my pores. I take hold of her jaw, pressing my fingers tight. "If he had only been a man and lived up to his word, his sweet little girl wouldn't have to go through this. Maybe after I take a few photos of you all splayed out and ready for me, I'll treat him to the sight of my cum dripping from your pussy. How do you think he'd like that?"

"He'll fucking kill you," she spits, and the fire in her eyes is so hot it could burn me alive.

"Will he, though? Or will he only wish he'd kept his word?" I can't help the smile that begins to stir my lips. "Of course, that will leave your honor destroyed. For some in our world, that still matters. I wonder if it matters to him. I wonder if he would ever be able to marry you off to anyone else once I make sure everybody knows I fucked every single one of your holes. When they know, I claimed you and defiled you for fun. What do you think would happen to you then? Do you think anyone would want you? Do you think you'll have any value in your family after that?"

It turns out she can still surprise me. Her gaze is cold, flat as she lifts an eyebrow. "Are you sure that's what would happen? Or are you telling yourself that as a way of excusing what we both know you want to do?"

I place a hand on either side of her head and lower myself until our bodies touch. "Can't it be both?"

She lets out one of those animal grunts and practically levitates off the bed, making us both bounce as she fights harder than ever.

I look down between us when I feel the tight little nubs rubbing against my chest. "Well, look at this," I murmur. "Somebody is getting excited."

"You're a pig."

"Yes, yes, I'm a pig." I reach between us and flick one of them, noting the way her jaw tightens. "The pig that's turning you on. What does that say about you, I wonder?"

"Leave me alone. Stop this."

"I don't want to. And if I'm going to be stuck with you, I might as well enjoy it." I flick the other nipple, and this time her nostrils flare along with that tightened jaw. It's clear she's fighting against what her body wants. "And it seems like you might enjoy it, too. Why deny yourself?"

"You don't know what you're talking about."

"You don't sound so sure anymore," I observe, twisting both nipples until she whimpers. It's different from before when I had her downstairs. She's not afraid, at least not of getting hurt. If anything, she's afraid of what this is doing to her, of reactions she can't control.

"I don't want this. I don't want you."

"Are you sure about that?" Now, instead of being almost cruel, I'm gentle, rubbing my thumbs in slow circles over those taut little peaks. She closes her eyes, a tear squeezing out from under her lashes. I catch it on the tip of my finger and place it on my tongue, savoring the taste.

She's stopped fighting, though the motion from her hips hasn't stopped.

"You're breathing faster," I observe. Now losing myself a little at a time with every soft gasp and strangled moan. I want to hurt her. I want to make her fall apart because of me.

"I wonder what's going on down here." I turn my attention further south, parting her thighs. She tries to clamp them shut, but I spread them again, this time placing myself between them so she has no hope of hiding herself from me.

"Stop it. Don't touch me there."

"The more you try to tell me what to do, the less choice I have. When are you going to learn that?" I glance up into her eyes. "Besides. You're only kidding yourself. We both know it."

"You're the one kidding yourself." She tries to kick, but I grab her ankle and place it on my shoulder, holding it there.

"Am I, though? I can smell your pussy already. I bet if I put my fingers in there, they'll come back coated in your juices. How much do you want to bet?"

She's vibrating with rage. "You fucking twisted asshole."

"Oh, don't tempt me. Has anyone ever taken that part of you before?" She squeezes her eyes shut, and I can only laugh.

Her body goes stiff, her breath picking up speed when I drag my fingers over her covered pussy. "Stop denying yourself," I murmur before pushing the fabric aside, baring her smooth sweetness to me. I can't resist. I don't want to resist. I slide a finger between her swollen lips—sure enough, she's soaking wet, glistening on my fingertip. "Relax and enjoy it. You know you want to."

"Stop..." it's the weakest whisper, so quiet I can barely hear.

I couldn't stop if I wanted to, not with my cock threatening to burst out of my pants and every nerve in my body singing, vibrating in anticipation. I probe her entrance, teasing her before pushing in a little farther.

Surprise widens my eyes and makes me forget some of the

urge to take her. This can't be. It's impossible. But I know what I'm feeling, the membrane blocking me from going any further. She's a virgin.

I haven't yet wrapped my head around that when my phone rings. I was so caught up in her that I almost forgot I was supposed to be using it to threaten her.

Nothing will kill an erection faster than the sight of my grandfather's name on the screen. I pick up the phone and climb off the bed but don't bother freeing her. We're obviously going to have to have a talk about a few things.

"Hello? What—"

"What the fuck do you think you're doing? When were you going to get around to telling me who you've been keeping with you all this time? What are you playing at?"

An icy finger moves up my spine and freezes my blood. Son of a bitch. How does he know?

I barely have time to process the question before the answer reveals itself. "You'd better hope you haven't harmed a single hair on her head!" Josef Alvarez howls. "How dare you? Who do you think you're dealing with? Is this all a fucking game to you?"

Can she hear any of this? I doubt I would be able to tell if she could—she looks just as terrified as ever. I'm sure she can tell I'm being reamed out, but if she knew exactly what her father was saying, she might look a little more pleased with herself than she does now.

"You're only finding out now?" I ask.

"Listen here," my grandfather growls. "This is not your time to ask questions. You have gone ahead and behaved recklessly without first clearing things with me. You and I will have this out later, mark my words. For now, we need to find a way to repair the damage you've done."

It's only because she's listening intently that I'm able to keep my temper under control. "The damage I've done? Who sent a sniper to what was supposed to be a meeting yesterday?"

"Renato, you finish this. I can't stand the sound of his voice any longer. But you listen here, boy," Alvarez adds. "I find out you've done a damn thing to harm what's mine, and any deal between our families is forgotten. Understood?" With that, he hangs up on his end, leaving only Grandfather and me.

"Listen," I implore, but he cuts me off with a growl.

"You listen, you reckless son of a bitch. You have no idea the scrambling it's taken to convince that man not to kill you outright. Thanks to me, it looks like we've come to an arrangement that will suit both of us just fine and cement the union between our families."

It's his choice of words that get my blood running cold again. "Tell me you aren't thinking what it sounds like you are thinking, please."

"It's time for you to learn what happens when you go off half-cocked and fuck with everything I've worked for. You're going to marry that girl, and you're going to do it soon. Only that will undo the damage you've done by going behind my back and thinking you make the decisions in this family. I have never been this disappointed in you, Enzo."

Maybe if I was a child, that last part would make any sort of difference. Maybe it would matter in the slightest that my grandfather feels disappointed.

However, I can't get past what he announced before that. "You're serious? You mean it?"

"I'm beginning to think Miami has softened your brain. Since when do I say anything I don't mean? You treat that girl with kid gloves between now and the wedding, or else I'll have no choice but to wash my hands of you. Don't force me to make that move. I promise you, you will regret it."

I can barely catch my breath before he hangs up, leaving me stunned and as close to helpless as I can remember ever feeling.

That bastard. This has to be what he was playing at all along. Taking the chance of leaving her with me, waiting to drop the bombshell on my grandfather's head. His way of uniting our families and benefiting from the arrangement more so than he could ever have hoped before.

She hasn't spoken a word, has hardly breathed. When I turn and fix a cold stare on her, she cringes.

"Congratulations," I grunt. "You're going to be married. To me." I can't even take pleasure in her horror.

15

ALICIA

I don't know what happened. I don't know how long I've been asleep—at some point, exhaustion finally caught up with me, and there was nothing to do but give in to it. Even if I wasn't dead tired, my body would have probably shut down if only to let me escape fear for a little while. There's only so much a human being can take. I'm starting to understand that in a way I never did before.

Now I'm awake, and everything comes rushing back. How could it not, with my arms still tied over my head? I've been this way for so long that they're numb. And he left me this way. Like I don't even matter.

His future wife, too. Fuck. I forgot about that for a minute. Was he kidding about getting married? Just when I thought I had faced every possible horror, he had to go and spring that on me.

The idea of being married to somebody like him turns my stomach. I think I'm trapped now? How much worse would it be with a marriage license involved? What's the play here? Why would he want to do this? Something tells me it's not his idea—he didn't look too happy about it when he announced it. More like it was something he has to do, something somebody is pushing him into.

Terrific. Because forced marriage never resulted in resentment, which I know would only make my life infinitely worse.

I should have told him the truth from the beginning. Why was I so stupid? I can't even remember the thought process that went on in my head when I decided not to come clean with who I really am. What was I so afraid of? I guess I can be forgiven for not being able to predict how much worse things would get.

Now here I am, unable to free myself, naked except for my panties. Humiliation makes me shudder. I could scrub my body raw, and I wouldn't be able to clean away the dirtiness I feel. The shame. I didn't do anything to deserve this. I was desperate, was all. And now I'm going to spend the rest of my life paying for it.

My heart lurches at the sound of approaching footsteps, and the soft squeal of the door hinges when Enzo opens it. "Oh, you're awake," Enzo mutters like I'm an afterthought. He looks more rested, not to mention showered and shaved. Lucky him, having the option of doing those things for himself.

It's enough to make my blood boil. "You just left me like this? How could you do that?"

He tips his head to the side, eyes narrowing. I don't even care anymore if he's pissed. I'm pissed, too. I did nothing to hurt him, but all he's done is abuse me from the start.

"Forgive me." Sarcasm practically drips from every word as he puts a hand to his chest. "I was unaware that scheming, traitorous little bitches who try to sneak out of my house while I'm asleep deserve special treatment."

"I'm not a traitorous little bitch."

"But you are a schemer."

"Would you stick around without at least trying to get away if you knew somebody was going to kill you?"

He has the nerve to scoff at this, approaching the bed. "Oh, spare me," he mutters when I tense up and even whimper in fear. "First, you complain that I tied you up, then you act like this when I come over to untie you. Make up your mind."

He's telling the truth, too, untying the shirt from the headboard, then removing it from my wrists. Right away, I have to bite back the pained groans that come immediately now that the blood is starting to rush back to my arms. My shoulders ache like hell, too, and soon the rush of pins and needles leaves me wincing and gritting my teeth.

He's still standing next to the bed, looking down at me with hunger in his eyes. No fucking way am I going to lie here and let him do what he's thinking of. "Excuse me," I mutter, sitting up, ignoring the soreness in my back. It's amazing I slept at all, being in such an awkward position the entire time.

"Where do you think you're going?" He comes closer to me, blocking my way.

"I was going to check on Prince," I explain, though that's more of an excuse to get away from him than anything else. "I haven't been in to see him since I stitched him up, remember?"

"Oh?" He folds his arms, smirking like the smug, sick bastard he is. "So all of a sudden, you give a shit about Prince? You were about to run away and leave him earlier tonight."

"Considering I'm still here, I figured it makes sense. Unless you don't care whether he's okay or not."

He snorts. "You don't have to worry about that. He's gone."

"Gone?"

"The doctor came while you were asleep," he explains. "He's getting that actual medical care you were talking about."

"Oh. Okay. That's good."

"I'm glad you approve," he snorts. He also doesn't back away even when I move like I'm trying to get up.

"What are you doing?" I finally have to ask with a sigh. "I have to go to the bathroom."

"Did I say you were allowed?"

Oh, for God's sake. He's going to make sure to punish me in every way he can think of. I could have gotten myself out of this if I had only been a little faster.

It's obvious what he's looking for. I hate giving it to him, but I can't sit here like this all night. "Can I please get up and go to the bathroom?"

"No. You're going to stay right where you are."

"What was that you said about not wanting to buy another mattress?" I get up anyway, even though there's hardly any space between him and the bed. When he tries to block me, I elbow him in the ribs.

I don't know why I did it. I'm just so tired of this. Tired of being afraid. Tired of never knowing what's happening next or which version of this psycho I'm going to meet.

But maybe, all things considered, I shouldn't have gone that route. Because now the psycho grabs me by the throat with one hand—then wedges the other between my thighs, grabbing my pussy hard enough that tears spring to my eyes.

"When are you going to learn?" He starts flat-out squeezing my throat, and the pressure in my head makes me sure it's going to explode. "I don't know who told you that you get a say in anything that goes on under my roof, but they were dead fucking wrong."

At least I'm able to breathe when he shoves me onto my

back, but it doesn't last long. He's on top of me again before I know it, again cutting off my air. "You belong to me." And like he wants to prove it, he takes hold of my pussy again, rubbing hard, brutally, laughing while I weep silently for lack of air.

"This pussy is mine. This body is mine." He's breathing hard, like a beast ready to go for the kill. "If you go anywhere, it's because I said you could go. If you stay, it's because I want you exactly where you are. Understood?"

I slap weakly at his hand, trying to remind him that I need to breathe if he wants me to live. The instant he eases up, I suck in a deep breath, choking and gagging.

"Answer me," he demands, pulsing his fingers, squeezing and releasing my throat until he drags a dismayed moan from between my lips.

"Understood," I gag out.

"I don't know if I believe you. How do I know you aren't only saying this to make me stop?"

"I mean it!" I sob. "Please!"

"Please, what?" Now he presses so tight against my pussy that it feels like he's going to tear through my panties. "Please take this sweet, fresh pussy? Is that what you're begging for?" He takes the waistband and starts pulling the panties down.

"No! No, please!" My voice is barely audible, not like he would listen. I slam my fists into his hands, his arms, his chest. It's like trying to punch steel.

"Now, what did I tell you?" he asks, pulling the panties over my feet and throwing them aside. "It only gets me hard when you fight like that. So which is it? Do you want me to stop, or do you want me to fuck you?"

"Stop!" I croak, even if I know it's not a genuine question. This is all another game. A game where I hold no cards. He has the entire deck.

"Are you sure you want me to stop?" He teases my lips, stroking them almost playfully and sending white-hot sizzles of pure, unbearable sensation racing through me from head to toe. It's never been like this, not in all the times I touched myself. Like I'm losing control of my body, like his touch is unlocking some part of me I didn't know existed.

"Well?" He's grinning, savoring my agony. "Are you sure you want me to stop? Because from where I am, it's feeling warm and wet down here. You should learn to make up your mind."

I'm so embarrassed. I would close my eyes even if the deepening pleasure of his touch didn't already make me close them. I want to enjoy this, to lose myself.

I want him to stop because this is humiliating, the way he knows how to undo me like this. It's not fair. It's disgusting and shameful. And if he stops, I'll die.

"That's right," he murmurs from somewhere far away, his voice barely a hum over the rush of blood in my ears. "Give up the fight. Take what you want."

But I don't want this. I want him to stop, to take his hands off me, to never touch me again. I want him to let me go. I want him to let me get on with my life, which I will never, ever complain about for any reason as long as I live. I want him to forget we ever met.

So that must be why my hips start rolling in circles, my pussy desperate for his fingers to go deeper, to touch me where I'm slick and throbbing. It actually hurts.

"Greedy," he observes with a nasty little laugh. I open my eyes just enough to look up at him—his eyes are half-lidded, his nostrils flared, and his mouth partly open as he takes one shallow breath after another. I am totally at his mercy, and I hate myself for loving it, for being so desperate for more.

The twitching of his lips tells me he sees that, that somehow, he knows, and my hatred for him only deepens even while my hips start jerking and a wet spot forms under my ass.

"You've been denying yourself for so long, haven't you?" His voice is surprisingly soft, almost crooning the words. "This sweet, pink little pussy. Nobody's ever touched it before me, have they? Nobody but you, I bet."

I squeeze my eyes tightly shut like that will blot out his voice, but it's no use. I hear him and his nastiness loud and clear. Even though it disgusts me and makes me hate myself for loving this so much, I can't help but react to what he's saying. It's nasty, but that only makes me burn hotter than ever.

"Did it ever feel this good before? When you were touching yourself in your room late at night?" I strain upward, hungry for what's building—because yes, of course, I've touched myself before. I know what it feels like when an orgasm is on the way, and oh, fuck me, it's on the way now.

He dips into my wetness, sweeping his fingers up the length of my slit, and I would scream if I could take a deep enough breath. The hand around my throat only makes this more intense. There's so much happening, almost too much. Almost enough to make me beg him to stop because I can't take anymore.

Almost.

"No man will ever touch this pussy but me. No man will ever make you feel this way but me. Because you're mine now. You belong to me." He grits it out through clenched teeth, and I wonder somewhere in the back of my overheated brain if he's taunting me or reminding himself. Maybe both.

He teases my entrance, and I gasp, going stiff, knowing what's coming next. He's going to put his fingers inside me before putting his dick in there. I don't want it like this. Not the first time. Not ever.

But he only teases me, pressing a little, then circling with his fingertip. It's torture, nothing less, the tension enough to break my brain. When will he let me come? I whimper under his hand, thrusting my hips in hopes he'll touch my clit, so I can finally get relief.

"You wanna come for me?" he whispers, squeezing my throat harder and making everything more intense than ever. My body jerks on its own, fighting for air but even harder to find release from this overwhelming torment. "Do you? Are you going to scream until you can't make a sound?"

"Yes!" I gasp, and I hate myself for it. For letting him do this to me, for making it so easy. I'm going to come, and when I do, I'm going to scream until my throat bleeds. I'm going to do all the screaming I haven't been able to do since I got here. I can't wait. It's so close... almost there... just a little more...

The world comes into sharper focus when the pressure on my throat goes away. It doesn't lessen. He flat-out lets go, just pulls his hand away from my pussy and leaves me hanging—writhing, whimpering, and almost weeping with frustration.

"What... why..." It comes out broken and gravelly, thanks to my aching throat. He laughs, shaking his head at me before climbing off the bed. What the hell? What's this new game? My entire body is screaming for relief, and he's crossing the room, walking to the door.

"What, feeling unfulfilled?" he mocks before laughing nastily again. "Poor baby."

"But—"

He shoots me a dark look over his shoulder that cuts off any question I might've wanted to ask. "We have to save something for the wedding night, don't we?"

BEAST

16

ENZO

$\mathcal{I}$'ve never so clearly understood what it means to wish I could go back and change everything. I suppose everyone goes through that at least once in their lifetime. Looking back on a decision they made that changed the course of their life. Wishing they would have chosen differently.

I should never have taken her. What seemed natural at the time, sensible, is the biggest mistake I've ever made.

And I'm going to be paying for it for the rest of my life.

I pace the house like a caged animal, kicking furniture aside and slamming my fists against the walls in passing. That bastard. I played straight into his hand, didn't I? I left the way wide open for him to slither in and make a place for himself in my family. I ruined everything, all because of a simple, thoughtless action.

All because of her. I can't remember now why it seemed necessary to take her from the warehouse. If only I had left her there, unconscious, none of this would be happening. I wouldn't have my grandfather threatening to destroy me. I wouldn't have left us open to a man like Alvarez, who only ever wanted to strengthen his position by using his daughter. Did she know? Has she been stalling all this time, confident in the knowledge he would eventually claim her and use her as a means of strengthening his family? I'm sure that's all she's ever been good for in his eyes, as it is. Someone to marry off. Here I am, the unwitting rube, thinking I could use her and have a little fun when really, they were all having fun with me. It just so happens I'm the last to find out about it.

"Motherfucker!" I slam the whiskey bottle onto the cart after filling a glass. I doubt there's enough in the bottle to blot out my rage and regret, but I can sure as hell try.

Married. We have to get married. Has she known all along? My god. All this time, has she known?

I don't know why it matters. I don't know why the question burns more intensely than the whiskey now burning its way through my chest. Pretending to be frightened, knowing she'd be safe in the end. I should kill her for it. That would show Alvarez who's in control, wouldn't it? The thought brings me a grim smile and the first semblance of peace since I took the phone call earlier. He would learn how dangerous it is to fuck with me.

The thought is enough to make me start for the stairs, prepared to make her regret thinking she can pull some shit like this without facing repercussions.

Something stops me, leaving me gripping the banister as I stare up into the hall. I know how it's going to go. How I'll start out wanting to punish her but quickly end up wanting to indulge in her even more. I don't know what it is about her, but she's managed to work her way into my brain, into my soul. Like a drug I can't kick, always in the back of my mind, promising relief. Peace. Everything I crave most. All the empty promises an addict struggles with that's what I wrestle with. And I can tell myself all I want that I'll know when to stop, that I'm in control, but I know it's a lie. A means of justifying my dark, primal desire. My weakness.

But oh god, how much do I want to watch her come? To see her unravel in front of me, to hear my name tumbling from her lips again and again. No man has ever done that to her, and oh, she's so eager. She can fight all she wants, can pretend and deny, but there's no denying her body's reaction.

She's a magnet, pulling me up the stairs. As much as I know I shouldn't, I also know I don't have a choice. I'll have to face her eventually. There's no running away from this—nor should there be. I put myself in this position. But I can't touch her. Not now, not until after the wedding. Her father probably knows she's untouched, and I have no doubt my grandfather would want proof of that, as well. He wouldn't want me marrying anyone he doesn't approve of, no matter how crucial it is to the future of our family.

Still, my feet are heavy as I climb the stairs, but my heart is heavier. I've never been someone who can live with being told what to do. I don't dance to anyone else's drum, only my own. Or so I've wanted to tell myself. Underneath all of that has always been the awareness of Grandfather's power over me. I can deny it all I want, but that makes it no less potent. After all, if I denied the presence of gravity, would I suddenly float away?

I did this. I put myself in this position, and now my hands are tied. Hands that are clenched in tight fists when I stand in the open doorway, gazing upon the woman who is now my bride-to-be.

She's curled up on her side, miserable if the pained expression she wears is any indication. I want to take my rage out on her. I want to tell her how much I regret the entire situation. I wish I could punish her. I wish I could comfort her.

One thing I know, or at least strongly suspect: she had no part in any of this. No one could look so miserable, so bewildered, and not mean it.

I enter the room, but she gives no hint that she notices or even cares. Have I finally broken her down? Has some of the fire finally fizzled out? Is she just as much a pawn in all of this as I now am? I wish I could ask her, but I don't know the words to use. I don't know how to express myself in any genuine, meaningful way.

Especially not when all I want to do is continue what I started before. Just the thought of it makes my pulse quicken. It's so easy to arouse a virgin. To make them moan and beg, to make them lose their breath and their sense of time and place in favor of sensations they've never indulged in before. It's one thing to touch yourself, but to be touched by someone else? Someone who knows their way around a woman's body?

The way I know how to touch hers. And I want to give her more that's the worst part. I want her to feel these things with me, only with me. I want her to look at me in wide-eyed wonder, breathless and hazy and unable to wrap her mind around what her body just went through.

The sudden brush of fingers against the back of my hand makes me jump, startled back into the present moment. I didn't know I drifted off as I stood beside the bed. I also didn't know I dug the nails of my left hand so deep into my palm that I broke the skin and am now bleeding.

But she noticed, and she touched my hand. And now she's looking up at me, concerned, brows drawn together, her mouth pulling downward at the corners. "You hurt yourself."

"It's not the first time." Why did I say that? And why

don't I pull my hand away before she can slowly loosen my fingers one at a time, her touch gentle and careful but determined.

"You'll have to wash this." She looks up at me. "Didn't you feel it?"

"No," I reply when I should say I was too busy imagining everything I wanted to do to you, but I keep that to myself as she finishes unclenching my fist and examines my palm.

"Why do you care?" I blurt out. "What's this about?"

"Why does it have to be about anything?" She looks genuinely confused, and that confusion rings out in her voice, as well.

"I've been nothing but an asshole to you from the beginning."

"And how far would I get by being an asshole right back to you?"

"You would have every right."

"I tried that, didn't I? I fought and cursed you, and look where it got me. Nowhere. And now, we're supposedly going to get married." When I scoff, she nods slowly. "I know. And I'm thinking to myself, what if there's a way we can get out of it? I'm sure you don't want to be married to me any more than I want to be married to you. No offense or anything, but I always thought I would have at least a small say in my future husband."

I don't have the heart to tell her she's been fooling herself all along. I have no doubt her father would have chosen her husband no matter what, but I'm willing to play along to hear the rest of what she has to say. For some reason, the sound of her voice soothes me.

"Maybe if we work together instead of me fighting against you, it will get me home sooner." She gets up on her knees and begins to strain upward toward me, and I realize with no small amount of surprise that she intends to kiss me.

And it feels right. So right that I take her face in my hands and pull her in to kiss her as hard as I can, smearing my blood on her cheek and not giving a damn. Not when her lips are as sweet as honey and as addictive as anything I've ever tasted.

Though even the sweetest lips wouldn't mean a thing if the woman they belonged to didn't kiss me back. That's not a problem with her—no, she grabs my shoulders and hangs on tight, matching every thrust of my tongue with a thrust of her own. I don't know if we're kissing or battling for dominance as we bruise each other's lips, as our teeth clash in our frantic, almost brutal fight to claim each other.

I have to touch her. I need to. I've run my hand down her cheek, noting the slickness under my palm, knowing I'm leaving a trail of blood behind. She must feel it, but she doesn't react, only pulling me down on top of her as she falls onto her back. I gladly follow, my hand now running over her throat and down to her chest. She moans into my mouth, arching her back, giving herself to me. Silently begging for more. I knew she would be like this. It's why I should have stayed away, why I couldn't possibly stay away. She makes me forget everything I thought I knew. Makes me question everything about myself. And I hate her for it almost as much as I want her.

I roll my hips and press my aching cock against her, and she clings to me tighter, digging her nails into my shoulders, lifting her hips to meet my pressure with her own. It's enough to make me want to forget everything, lose myself in her, and never come back.

And I would, too. I would give up the fight and give in to the inevitable.

If it wasn't for the ringing of my phone. Yet again, I find

myself caught between what I want and what I know is the right decision. It's not like the man will let me get away with ignoring his call.

I pull back with a sinking heart and finally take in the sight of her covered in my blood, smeared from her cheek down to her tits.

I wish the sight didn't thrill me so much.

BEAST

17
ALICIA

I guess it's a good thing we were interrupted, even if, once again, my body feels like it's dangling at the edge of a cliff. Am I ever going to get the relief I'm craving?

I absolutely should not want that relief from him, so why do I? I never thought of myself as being desperate before. If I was desperate, I wouldn't still be a virgin. It never seemed worth it to me, especially since I had never met a man who interested me for very long. It was almost enough to make me wonder what was so different about me when other girls my age got laid all the time. I wondered if I was too picky or just afraid to go all the way.

Now, when I should be afraid more than anything else, all I want is for him to have his way with me. It's sick.

And when I look down at myself, at the blood he smeared on me, that feeling only intensifies. There's got to be something wrong with me for liking this. If for nothing else, I hate that he's brought out this side of me. I resent him for it.

With him out of the room, I get up and go to the bathroom to wash up. I can hear him talking on the phone, even if I can't make out the words. I don't need to make them out to know he's angry—extremely. This has to be the person who called and told him we were getting married. From what little I heard when he first answered the call, it was clear the voice belonged to a man. His father? Maybe a grandfather. Either way, whoever it is has a lot of power over him.

It's almost enough to make me wonder what their secret is because I could use a little bit of that power for myself. I'm tired of always being the one fighting for every inch of ground.

Every swipe of the warm washcloth reminds me of how the blood got there. When he ran his hand down my chest. Over my boobs. My neck. It's enough to tighten my nipples just thinking about it. I'm going to need a load of therapy after this, that much is obvious. It makes me angry, and I finish washing quickly before throwing the cloth into the hamper.

Once I'm dried off, I go downstairs to where Enzo is on the phone in the kitchen. He's washing his hand, cleaning where he made himself bleed. He doesn't acknowledge my presence, too busy grunting into the phone. "Yes," he mutters. "I know. I get it—you don't have to keep explaining it to me." He's fighting as hard as he can not to show his temper. There's no reason I should know that, really, but I can tell. I guess that's thanks to spending the past few days with him, watching him fight that temper when he's dealing with me. I sort of wish he'd fight a little harder is all.

Then he begins pacing the room, his hand wrapped in a dish towel while he holds the phone in the other. His knuckles stand out, bone white against his skin because he's clutching it so hard.

It's strange, the impulse that washes over me. I want to find a way to comfort him—it's stupid, but it's no more stupid than anything going on so far. Considering I've already come close to begging this man to take my virginity, this is nothing. Decency, that's all. Because I sort of feel sorry for him now. He seems a lot more human when he's on the receiving end of whatever verbal abuse he's getting from the man on the phone.

My empty stomach reminds me it's been a while since I've eaten anything resembling a meal. Maybe that will help—if I fix us both a little something. I need to establish a relationship with him where we're on equal footing. It's probably beyond naïve to think that will ever happen, but I need to do my best. The longer he thinks of me as his captive, the less likely it will ever be for me to get out of this. I have to believe there's still hope. Just because somebody told Enzo we're getting married doesn't mean it needs to happen. He has to have some say in it, doesn't he? Once he starts looking at me as an actual person with an actual life of my own, it might make him less likely to go through with this.

I need to believe that, even if it's hopelessly childish. Otherwise, I'm going to lose it.

One problem: I can't really cook. I start opening the cabinets to look around and see what's available—maybe cereal? There's plenty of food in the fridge, but I'm not even very good at cooking eggs. They always end up coming out overdone and rubbery, and I can never seem to get all the bits of shell out. What good is fixing something for him if it's disgusting? So that's not going to work.

The only thing I can think to make that's actually hot and hearty is the instant oatmeal sitting on one of the shelves. It's sort of pitiful, but it's the best I can do. There's a tea kettle on the stove that doesn't look like it's ever been used, almost like it's there for show. I can't imagine this man making himself a cup of tea. I rinse it out before filling it, put it on a burner, and turn it to high heat. It takes a minute for me to find the bowls, the silverware, all of that—so by the time I have a packet of oatmeal in each bowl, the water is beginning to boil, and a high-pitched squeal fills the air.

Enzo comes back from pacing the living room, scowling at me. I lift the kettle from the burner and shrug, but that seems to satisfy him. He goes back to his pacing, this time walking the kitchen while I pour water into the bowls. He's still not saying much, and I have to wonder if that's because the person on the other end never stops talking. Either that, or he knows better than to put up an argument. There I was, imagining him as somebody powerful, the sort of person who doesn't let anybody tell them what to do. I guess everybody has somebody higher up on the food chain who they need to answer to.

I place the bowls on the table and gesture for him to sit down. He's either too distracted by his conversation to question me, or he's genuinely hungry. Either way, he takes a seat, and I slide his bowl a little closer.

And all he does at first is stare at it, open-mouthed. Then he looks at me with plain confusion written all over his face. Okay, so maybe he's not interested in eating, or just doesn't care for instant oatmeal. Though I have to wonder why he'd have it in the cabinet if that's how he feels. Maybe it's just confusion in general. Why am I trying to take care of him, that kind of thing?

"You should eat," I whisper, taking a seat across from him and picking up my spoon. When he continues to stare like he's confused, I very deliberately take a spoonful of oatmeal and raise it to my lips. It's like I'm trying to teach a child to feed himself.

"I understand," he mutters, forgetting about me in favor of appeasing the person on the other end. I'm insanely curious now. Who are they? Why do they have this grip on him? How could I even ask that question in a way that would get me an answer? Is it worth trying? Do I really need to satisfy my curiosity?

I think it might be worth it. Until now, we've been nothing but adversaries. What if I make it so it seems like we're in this together? Just two people at the mercy of others, unable to make decisions for ourselves, unable to be free. Like Stockholm Syndrome in reverse, come to think of it. Could I use that to my advantage? I need to try. Otherwise, the alternative is getting closer to him until I end up identifying with him for real, becoming like an accomplice in this insanity. I can't let that happen. There is a world of difference between this man and me. I refuse to see it any other way.

So I'll pretend to be friendly. I'll try to reach the part of him that's isolated, alone, and maybe even helpless. God knows I understand that feeling. He's pretty good at hiding it, but when he's on the phone like this, and it's obvious he doesn't have the upper hand, that helplessness is written all over his face.

His eyes snap up from the bowl, locking onto mine, and I have no choice but to avert my gaze. I don't want him knowing I'm watching so closely. He might get suspicious. I eat slowly, taking my time, hoping to understand something, anything coming from the other side of the call. It's unnerving knowing they're talking about me even if Enzo doesn't refer to me by name. Whoever he's talking to, they're making plans for my future while I sit here and stir a bowl of oatmeal, quickly getting clumpy and cold.

"I don't think that will be a problem," he murmurs. I glance up at him from under my eyelashes and find him smirking. "Yeah, that's under control." A nasty little shiver runs up my spine at the tone in his voice. I have to fight the impulse to look up at him. I know he'd be able to read my thoughts since I've never been very good at keeping a poker face.

Once he gets off the phone, I'll have to be sympathetic. Can I pretend that well? He's so shrewd—it's almost impossible to get anything past him. Considering my life, my future, everything is hanging in the balance, I have no choice but to pretend. As dangerous as it is to think of him as a human being, it's what I have to do if I'm going to make this believable.

How does a person end up like him? I've seen good things from him. He was kind to me. Gentle. He could have used me in any way he saw fit when I was falling apart in his arms, but he chose instead to calm me down and be kind and wash me up without asking for anything in return. Deep down inside, there's a grain of decency in him. I need to focus on that.

And the person he's talking to, the one who gets him so worked up and intense. I'm sure they make him feel small and powerless, and nobody wants to feel that way. He's just as trapped as I am. What would I want him to say to me in this situation? What would make me feel better?

On second thought, no. He'll see through that. And he'll probably be more pissed than ever that I'm patronizing him or something. So I can't take it too far. Just a little sympathy, a little understanding.

As I sit here plotting, there's always that little reminder in the back of my head that this could all be over very quickly if I would just tell the truth. It's still too risky. He could kill me flat out, angry with himself for being fooled. He's the one who made the assumption that I'm part of this rival family or whoever they are. I'm sure he wouldn't like finding out how wrong he was. If he even believed me—and it's still possible he wouldn't. Would I if I were in his shoes? *Gee, how convenient, after all this time, you're finally going to tell me the truth? Why didn't you tell me before? Are you only lying yet again to save your hide?*

My stomach churns and threatens to send back the oatmeal I've shoveled into my mouth. Something tells me things would get ugly. So honesty is out, too.

"Fine." He shifts in his chair, and I look up in time to find him clenching his jaw. His nostrils are flared, his eyes narrowed, and his mouth twisted in disgust. "I said fine. I heard you. It's taken care of." Then he pulls the phone from his ear, smashes his finger against the screen, and slams it onto the table hard enough to make the spoon jump in his bowl. I can't help but flinch.

He doesn't say a word for a long time, which of course, doesn't comfort me very much. I wish he would say something, anything just so I know he's not going to explode on me. I'm afraid to breathe too loud in case that's what sets him off. For some reason, every time he has a conversation with this person, all it does is infuriate him. He was almost being normal for a little while there until the phone rang, and his mood swung back to this sullen, unpredictable version of himself.

"Are you okay?" I finally whisper after what feels like an eternity passes in silence.

"Of course I am," he mutters. "Why do you care?"

"I don't know. Because you seemed upset. Do you… want to talk about it?"

He goes from staring at the wall to staring at me like I'm something he's never seen before. It's enough to make my skin crawl, but I force myself to take it without reacting.

"What, we're friends now?" he scoffs, shaking his head. "I'd be in pretty bad fucking shape if I had to go to you for advice."

At least he's not threatening me or anything like that, but the cruelty behind his words hurts just the same. Like he's so much better than me? Where does he get off?

Steady, girl. Right. I can't afford to let my temper ruin things for me. I'm already screwed as it is.

"I'm just saying. It seems like whenever you talk to whoever that is, they end up upsetting you. I'm sorry that keeps happening."

"Yeah, I'm sure your heart is breaking for me," he mutters before snickering. "I'm sure it keeps you up at night, wondering if poor Enzo is doing okay after a phone call from his grandfather."

Now I know for sure who it is if only so I can keep things clear in my head. I hate the feeling of never knowing who I'm dealing with. "It doesn't keep me up at night. A lot of other things do, though."

"Yeah, I'm sure they do." He ignores the bowl in front of him, standing and pocketing his phone. "Hurry up. Finish eating so I can put you back in your room."

My heart sinks, and I can't hide it. "Really?" I ask with a sigh. "Do we have to keep doing that?"

"Last time I checked, I let you walk around here freely, and you tried to run away. What, I'm supposed to trust you now?" Before I can come up with a defense, he shakes his head. "It doesn't matter. I have to go out and deal with some things, so it's not like I would leave you unlocked anyway."

So much for my brief bit of freedom. I'm finished eating, so I take the bowls from the table and put them in the sink. That's as far as I'm willing to go. I'm not the maid. He doesn't seem to care—all that matters is getting me locked away so he can take care of business. Which is exactly what I'm sure my life would be like if we were ever married. I would be an afterthought, somebody to tuck away somewhere while he lived an actual life.

And I don't care how good it feels to be touched by him or how he seems to know exactly how to undo me.

I am never, ever going to let that happen.

BEAST

18

ENZO

"I have his strict assurance this time. No fucking around. No leaving you hanging."

All my grandfather's assurance makes me do is laugh bitterly from my seat in the car. "Sure. Why would he go back on his word now? He has exactly what he wanted."

"You gave him exactly what he wanted, remember? By taking his daughter in the first place."

I wish I could explain it in a way he would understand, but I doubt it would be possible no matter how hard I tried. He wasn't on the phone with the man when we set up that second meeting, the supposed face-to-face meeting at the hangar. The man was enraged and frantic, and he couldn't stop going on and on about me taking what belonged to him. How much he needed it back, how I would pay for what I had done.

Then he turned around and decided to use her as a pawn. He wanted her back, but then he didn't. And he still doesn't—this meeting is supposed to be a means of setting the terms for how we'll move forward. Either he was pretending all along, or somebody put this idea in his head. After all, he had already struck the first blow by not appearing at the warehouse. It could be that one of the more intelligent, levelheaded members of his crew suggested he use Elena's kidnapping to his advantage rather than huffing and puffing and threatening to blow the penthouse down.

It doesn't matter, really. I don't trust the man. I never will. And I'm about to step into a restaurant with him and make nice when I would prefer to lodge a bullet in his skull.

"Keep that temper of yours under control, and we are home free," Grandfather assures me. "We hold all the cards here, remember. He needs us much more than we need him, but this is a good alliance. Perhaps one of the best we could hope for. Do not fuck this up."

"I'll do my best."

"From what you've shown me lately, your best may not be good enough."

I close my eyes and force myself to take a deep breath before the temper he just acknowledged flares to life and gives me no choice but to tell him exactly what I think of him and this entire situation. I respect the man, but that doesn't mean I have to agree with him or his methods.

"Very well. I'll report when it's over." After ending the call, I look to my left, where one of the guards' Grandfather vouched for waits behind the wheel of the car. He kills the engine while the two men behind me exit the vehicle and do a quick check of the surrounding area before signaling that it's safe for me to leave the car. There's no avoiding flashbacks to Prince's shooting as I climb out. At least now I know I have men watching my back.

Besides, it's in Alvarez's best interest to leave me alive and well. He can't marry his daughter off to a corpse, can he?

The restaurant sits in a strip of similar establishments, all of which are in the process of opening for the evening within the hour. Behind the plate glass windows, staff members rush around, setting up tables and making sure the bar is well stocked. I've been down here at night more than once and have enjoyed myself immensely. Never would I have imagined the day I'd visit to meet with my future father-in-law during one of those drunken nights.

I step inside and notice this is the only restaurant without staff running around. Aside from the four men guarding him, Alvarez sits alone at a table, his hands folded atop the white tablecloth. In his linen suit and blood-red shirt, he makes quite the impression.

"Mr. Alvarez." I approach with my hand outstretched, but I'm quickly swarmed by his men.

"Stand down." He laughs. I recognize his voice, if not the humor in it. "The man is going to marry my daughter soon. I think we can trust him." Still, as a show of faith, I open my jacket to prove I'm not armed before the men step away and allow me to take a seat opposite their boss. He shakes my hand without rising, then folds them again before looking me up and down.

I make no effort to hide the way I do the same. When it comes to his attitude, his bearing, his command of the situation, he's precisely what I would have expected. This is not his first such meeting. He's been in the business for decades—his entire life, in fact. I have no doubt he was trained from an early age as I was.

Finally, it occurs to me. He doesn't bear much of a resemblance to Elena. His hair is black and wavy, his eyes the color of fresh coffee while hers are the most brilliant green. Nothing about his sharp features or his wiry frame suggests any relation to the girl I left at the townhouse. Nose, chin, ears—all different. She must take after her mother. Lucky girl.

"What would you like to drink? I've been assured the bar is open to us." He waves over one of his men and asks for a vodka and lime. I ask for a whiskey on the rocks before turning my attention back to Josef, whose thin lips twitch as if he finds something about this funny.

"I'm glad we can finally sit down together." I settle back in my chair, noticing from the corners of my eyes the way my men take their place beside me as Alvarez's men do the same. Let them do the sneering and posturing. The two of us have business to attend to.

"It seems we've gotten off to a rocky start, and I would like to apologize for the part I played in this situation. I ought to have reached out to you as soon as I knew I would be unable to make our first meeting. We could have rescheduled and avoided all of this."

"I admit," I murmur, "it came as a surprise."

"I'm sure it was nothing compared to the surprise I received when I learned my daughter was in your possession. I'm sure I don't have to tell you the anguish this has caused her poor mother."

"You have my apologies for that. It was never my intention to cause your wife strain." God, this is brutal. All this doubletalk, dancing around the subject when what I want to do is demand he tell me what the hell he thought he was doing, jerking me around the way he did. And now I'm supposed to feel sorry for his wife? This is all his fault.

At least, mostly. I would never have taken Elena if he'd been at the warehouse the way he said he would.

"How is she? She had better be unharmed."

"She is."

"I'll need to see her as proof of this before the wedding."

I keep my tone even, holding his gaze as our drinks arrive. "I'm sorry, but that's not going to happen."

"You won't allow me to see my daughter?"

"You can see her on the day of the wedding, but that's it. There won't be any meetings between you before then. I was assured by my grandfather that this was an acceptable condition to set."

"Oh, were you?" He lifts his glass, eyeing me as he drinks.

"Indeed, I was."

He lowers the glass, lips pursed. "Then there can be no deal."

"You're willing to blow up this entire deal because you can't see your daughter before the wedding? Is that really worth ending this over?"

"She deserves the opportunity to discuss the terms she wishes to set—with me, her father. We ought to at least be given the chance to speak privately, so I know what she wants."

"You can go through me."

"I will do no such thing."

I lift a shoulder. "Then we have no deal. And remember, this is Renato De Luca speaking, not me. I'm only relaying what he's already told me. You will not see her face-to-face before the day of the wedding, nor will you be afforded the opportunity for a private phone call. But you can communicate with me as a go-between."

"You De Lucas think you can control everything, don't you?" He sneers, leaning back in his chair. "What if I say no? What if this leads to an all-out war?"

"Is it worth that much to you? Having to reach a compromise, I mean?" I lean in, arms folded on the table. "Because if it does, my family already has more than enough reason to go to war. For starters, the man your sniper shot and nearly killed when we were supposed to be getting together for a meeting. You realize I brought her with me. She could have been killed."

"She was with you?"

I blink, trying to understand him. "You said you wanted what I took from you. Why would I not bring her with me?"

He frowns—then shrugs, his arms spread. "What can I say? It was a misunderstanding. An issue with communication. These things happen."

"You nearly took out one of my men. Is that one of those things that simply happens?"

"Since it did, I'd say yes. It happens." He lowers his brow. "You might want to watch before you step too far outside your boundaries."

One of the men standing at my side grunts, shifting his weight from one foot to the other like he's ready to remind the man to be respectful. Of course, that only inspires Alvarez's men to make a move like they're about to reach for their guns. I hold up a hand, shaking my head. "None of that will be necessary," I murmur. "No violence here. We wouldn't want to ruin the union of our families before the wedding even takes place. All of this will have been for nothing, and my poor fiancée will be left without a husband. Or a family."

He recoils slightly but maintains his composure. "Stand down," he mutters, and I have to hold back a grin. He's not a stupid man, even if he makes unfortunate decisions like double-crossing me.

"Back to the matter at hand. I arrived at the agreed-upon location in good faith, and you tried to kill me. Who overstepped their boundaries—with all due respect?" I add with a faint smile.

Color rises in his cheeks, and his eyes narrow. "Very well. I'm tired of running around in circles over this. I have other things to take care of."

Yes, I'm sure making certain his daughter is safe and well is a real inconvenience. "So you agree, then? You don't see her until the day of the wedding?"

He grits his teeth, and I can't pretend it isn't gratifying. He's holding no cards here. If he wants to make a deal and solidify his family's position, he has no choice but to agree. I could sit here all day and watch him pretend he isn't squirming. I'm enjoying my drink.

Finally, he grunts. "I see her before the wedding, and we will confirm the terms then. Before any vows are exchanged."

"Fair enough. I believe we can agree on that." Now he looks like he wishes he'd asked for more since I agreed so quickly. He doesn't understand that I wouldn't have agreed to more than that. Grandfather already gave me the terms, and I've no choice but to adhere to them. No matter how much I'd rather tell him to fuck himself while his daughter watches.

"What sort of wedding do you have in mind?" he asks.

"Something small. Simple. A few witnesses."

"You don't think my daughter deserves better than that?"

"How much are you willing to pay?" I ask with a smile that lands like a knife to his chest if the way he grimaces means anything. "Let's be frank. The point of this is to exchange vows and place our names on a marriage license. Anything more than that is unnecessary. If you disagree, your lovely wife is more than welcome to plan the sort of wedding her little girl deserves."

"No." It's too sharp, too sudden. "No, there's no need for that."

"Very well. Whatever you prefer." Because he doesn't give a

shit, and he doesn't care about his daughter's so-called terms. I wonder if he knows how easy it is to see through him. "Was there anything else you wanted to discuss, sir?"

"No. I think that will do it. I assume the day your grandfather set is to your liking?"

"One day is as good as any other—as soon as possible, of course," I add with a wide smile as we both stand. "I'm not sure how much longer I can wait before making your daughter my wife."

"Yes," he replies with just as wide a smile. "I can hardly wait for that day, myself. Nor can I wait for our families to join."

I'm sure he's chomping at the bit.

Our handshake is firm but brief, and I have to resist the impulse to wipe my hand on my jacket as I turn away. That was easier than I imagined.

Though something is stuck in my craw, and it doesn't hit me until I'm in the car.

He was too happy. Almost gleeful. I can't imagine why.

BEAST

19

ALICIA

I'm pretty sure I'm going to go crazy. Being in this room, alone and locked in. The entire time Enzo was out of the house, I couldn't stop worrying. What if there was a fire? I doubt I could make it through the window—if I could even reach the window in the first place. I wouldn't have any way of getting help, either. No phone in here, no way for me to even call the fire department.

At least, all's well that ends well when it comes to that. He came home after what was probably a few hours, and I heard him moving around the house before he stopped in and left me a change of clothes and some food.

But he never looked at me. He never even said a word, leaving just as suddenly as he came in. I don't get him. How can he treat me like, I don't know, a piece of furniture or something? I wouldn't even treat a pet the way he treats me. I would at least make sure they weren't locked away, alone, with no way to take care of themselves.

Now it's the middle of the night. The sense of never knowing the exact time is wearing on me, too. By the time I give up the fight and stop trying to fall asleep, there's faint birdsong coming from outside. We must be getting close to morning.

If it wasn't for the noise coming from somewhere else on this floor, I wouldn't get out of bed and go to the door. I wouldn't knock or call his name. "Enzo?" I jiggle the doorknob, which of course, doesn't do anything but make more noise. When I don't get an answer right away, I knock again. "Where are you? I need you."

The lock clicks after a few seconds, and I step back from the door as he swings it open.

It takes a moment for me to realize what I'm looking at. The hallway is dark, so I don't make him out clearly right away.

But once I do, my heart seizes, and my face flushes because he's naked. Completely, totally bare from head to toe.

He's also groggy, looking at me through squinted eyes. "What is it?" he mumbles.

Damned if the sight of his naked body didn't make me forget everything I've ever known. I doubt I could come up with my own name if somebody put a gun to my head. "Uh... I mean..."

"Come on. Out with it. I don't have all day."

"I can't sleep," I finally blurt out, forcing myself to stop staring at his abs, his chest, his dick. I don't have a lot of experience with them, but even I can tell it's pretty big even when it's soft like it is now. I can't stop glancing at it.

"And?" he prompts, either not noticing the way I can't stop peeking at him or not caring.

It's easier to snap out of it when he acts this way. "I was wondering if I could go downstairs and make something warm to drink."

He lifts an eyebrow before rubbing his eyes, then scrubs his hands over his hair. It was already sort of sticking up in different directions when he came to the door so that only makes it worse. "Something warm?"

"Don't act like you've never heard of people doing that before." I can't help but get a little exasperated when he lifts a shoulder. Is he putting this on for show just to make me feel stupid? He must be. "You know, like warm milk. I'm sure you've seen people do it on TV, or in movies at least."

"Yeah, maybe," he mutters, waving a hand. "I guess so. Go ahead."

Wow. That was easier than I expected.

But of course, there are always strings attached. In this case, he leads the way, and I have no choice but to follow him down the stairs. He hasn't bothered to put any clothes on, which is either a good thing or a bad thing depending on how I look at it. And I need to not look at it. That's the whole problem. The way I want to look at him, all of him, for as long as possible.

I really, really wish I had a little more experience with sex. Maybe it wouldn't seem like such a big deal to be walking around the house with a naked man if I had seen more naked men in real life. Is there ever a time when something like that becomes commonplace?

I doubt it ever could when the man in question looks like him. He's practically superhuman. Like a photoshopped image come to life.

Once we reach the kitchen, and he turns on the light over the stove, I have no choice but to stop staring since he turns around and gives me a challenging sort of look. "Well? Go ahead. Make your warm drink."

I swear he couldn't be more sarcastic about it if he made air quotes with his fingers.

"Where are the pots?" He points at one of the cabinets under the counter, and I find a small one that I set on the stove. There's milk in the refrigerator, and I pour roughly a cup worth of it into the pan—before adding more for him. Meanwhile, he busies himself, grabbing a bottle of water, then leans against the counter and takes a deep swig.

So he's going to stand there completely naked while I do this. Fine. I can handle myself. No big deal. At least the fear of letting the milk boil over will be enough to keep me focused. There's nothing worse than burnt milk. Something tells me he wouldn't like it very much, either.

"Spices?" I ask, turning to him.

"Spices?"

"You know. This stuff you sprinkle on food to make it taste good?"

"What do you need them for?"

For God's sake, it's like pulling teeth. "I just want some cinnamon. That's it. Do you have any?"

It's almost funny how he looks around like he's unaware of his own kitchen. I'm of half a mind to ask if he just moved in last week, but I can't press my luck. Finally, he opens a drawer and reveals rows of small bottles clearly labeled with their contents.

"Thank you." I pull out the cinnamon, uncap it and take a sniff. When I can't help but smile, he notices. "Does cinnamon make you happy?"

"In a way, yes. It brings back good memories." The milk is just starting to bubble, so I turn off the heat and move the pot over to a cold burner. When I turn to him, brows lifted, he opens a cabinet to reveal glasses and mugs. I pulled down two and pour an equal amount of milk into both.

"My mom used to make this for me when I was little," I explain, shaking a couple of dashes of cinnamon on top of both mugs before stirring a little. Then I slide one of the mugs his way before taking a sip for myself. Again, I smile as countless happy, peaceful memories come rushing back. It's almost enough to make me want to cry when I think of how normal my life used to be before I made the one terrible, game-changing decision that landed me here.

"When you couldn't sleep?" he asks, and I have the pleasure of watching him pick up his mug and sniff like he didn't just watch me prepare the damn thing from beginning to end. What, does he think I slipped poison in there? I take another sip, hiding my grin while he takes an experimental sip of his own.

"That's pretty good," he admits like he's surprised.

"It always did the trick. I don't know if the milk itself had anything to do with it or the ritual. But I never had a hard time falling asleep after we shared some warm milk in the kitchen, just the two of us."

"That sounds pretty nice." He says it like it comes as a surprise. I can only imagine somebody like him looking down on so-called normal people and their normal lives. Maybe it does surprise him that there's something to be said for those of us who lived quiet, average lives.

I have to take a chance, both because he's being quiet and thoughtful and because I'm insanely curious about this man. "What about you?" I venture.

He frowns. "What about me?"

"Did your mom ever do stuff like that for you when you were little? To help you sleep, or when you were sick?"

He stares down into the mug, and I think I asked the wrong question. It's so tough to figure out how much is too much with him. But he doesn't lash out at me or shut me down the way I expect him to. "I wasn't raised by my mother. My grandfather raised me."

The back of my neck tingles, but I have to ignore it to focus on him. Maybe I'll finally get some answers to all the questions bouncing around in my head. "I see."

"No, you don't," he tells me with a smirk. "My mother… died when I was really young. Or rather, she was killed."

I can't breathe for a second; it hits me so hard. Not just the revelation, but the way he reveals it in a flat, almost lifeless voice. I wonder how hard he's had to work to suppress his feelings about her death that he's able to just rattle it off like he's totally unconnected from the words he's saying.

"I'm so sorry," I whisper. And I am, extremely so. But I don't want him getting upset and thinking I'm going overboard to kiss up to him. I wish everything I did or said didn't feel like a chess move I have to plan out in advance. It's maddening.

He shrugs a little, taking another sip of the milk. "And my grandfather… He's not the kind of guy who would sit up with me late at night and make me warm milk to help me sleep." His lips twitch like the very idea is too funny to even consider.

"Was he good to you, at least?"

"Oh, don't get the wrong idea. I'm not some poor little orphan. I made out just fine. But it's times like this…" He stares down at the milk, frowning. "I remember there are things I missed out on."

"Do you remember anything about her?"

He shakes his head a little. "Honestly, no. I was very little when she died."

"I really am sorry." No wonder he is how he is. Hard, brittle, brutal. The man whose phone calls make him so angry is the man who raised him. From what I've witnessed so far, it couldn't have been a very cheerful upbringing. I doubt there was very much fun for him as a kid. And he probably never felt like he could be a little kid—*be a man, boys don't cry*, that kind of thing.

Right now, I don't see the man in front of me. I'm not even paying attention to his body, not very much anyway—it's kind of hard to ignore completely. But what I see more than anything is a little boy who never knew his mom, who was raised by a man who to this day rides him incessantly. What must that have been like? Did he ever get a hug? I want to hug him now.

It's dangerous letting myself think of him this way. I know it. I have to be careful, right?

He offers the briefest of apologetic smiles. "You didn't ask for my life story."

"But I'm here. And I'm not doing anything else, am I?"

He laughs a little at this, nodding before draining the rest of his milk. "That's true. But still. I don't like to talk about it."

"I understand." And I really do. I'm not just saying that to get closer to him or whatever. If there was ever an example of what happens to a person when they're not allowed to feel things, it's the man standing in front of me. Now I understand a little better those tiny glimpses of kindness that pop up now and then and how he quickly suppresses them or suddenly swings in the opposite direction and acts brutal and cruel. Maybe he was raised to think it was weak to feel things, to be kind. But his nature is another story. It wants to get out.

What am I doing? Humanizing him? Identifying with him? I might as well hand over my entire life at this point. I'm making it easy for him to dominate me, making up excuses in my head.

He leaves his mug in the sink, and I do the same, feeling a little awkward now. I don't know if he feels the same way or if he just wants to put an end to this, but he clears his throat. "Come on. I need to get some sleep."

I guess that's his way of saying I have to get back to bed, too. I am tired, though. Whether it's psychosomatic or not, the milk has relaxed me. I feel myself unwinding, my eyelids drooping a little as I climb the stairs.

He waits until I'm in bed, standing in the doorway. "Good night." It feels funny hearing that when it'll be morning pretty soon, but I murmur the same thing before resting my head on the pillow.

And when he closes the door, there is no clicking sound this time. He didn't lock it.

20

ENZO

"So help me God, don't make me regret this." I unlock the passenger side door but hold her against the car before she can get in. "I mean that. Do not make me regret doing this."

"I won't, I promise." As it is, she's a little wide-eyed and shaken by my sudden announcement. I supposed it must have come as a shock that I'd want to take her shopping.

It's a purely self-serving decision. I can't have her walking around in my clothes all the time, and not only because she's so damn tempting in them. What is it about a woman wearing oversized clothes that's such a turn-on? She manages to look sexy, adorable, even.

And I can't keep my eyes off her, to say nothing of my hands. I spent far too much time lying in bed after leaving the kitchen thinking about her, envisioning her holding a cup of milk with cinnamon sprinkled on top, dressed in an oversized shirt, and looking sweet and vulnerable.

Now isn't the time to think about that. I have to be firm with her, as this is a huge risk. "If you so much as hint to anyone around us that you need help for any reason, it's over." I open the door and usher her inside, wasting no time getting behind the wheel. I don't even want to give her an extra few seconds with the car door unlocked. The moment I'm inside, I slam the door and activate the locks.

"What do you mean it's over?" She's practically hugging the door, clearly nervous. Good. If she's nervous, she'll be less likely to do anything stupid. I wouldn't trust her if she acted confident right now.

"It means I'll chain you to the bed, naked, and you'll stay there until our wedding day. Understood?"

Her head bobs up and down. "Understood."

"Good." I still have the feeling I'm going to regret this, but there's no way around it. She needs things, including something to wear for our wedding.

Our wedding. I still can't wrap my head around that. The thought of it leaves a bad taste in my mouth as I back out of the driveway and pull out of the development. Our wedding. I'm going to have to marry this woman.

The worst part is that I don't feel nearly as bitter about that as I did before. And that's dangerous, too. I can't deny the fact that she's growing on me. Moments like this morning in the kitchen, the two of us talking quietly, sharing bits of our past. That can't be, it mustn't be, but it happened. And it was so damn easy. We started talking, and I relaxed, and all of a sudden, I was saying things I've told hardly anyone. Almost no one knows about my mother, about how I came to live with my grandfather. I'll be damned if anyone sees me as the poor little motherless boy.

But she does. I saw it in her eyes, in the pained expression she wore. I saw pity.

I'm not a man to be pitied.

I'm also not a man she wants to get close to. Not if she hopes to live very long. That's what plagues me worst of all as I pull onto the freeway and head downtown. I don't know anymore if I'm pushing her away because I don't want her or because it would be safest for her to stay far away from me. I'm the last man she needs to develop any sort of tender feelings toward.

All I'll do is get her killed the way my mother was. She deserves better than that. She deserves better than me, for sure. Considering the man who fathered her, I'd say she's already suffered more than enough. I can't imagine how he's treated her, and I'm not sure I want to know. Not when it would be so easy to murder the bastard. Maybe once we're back in Italy, with an ocean between him and us, I can satisfy my morbid curiosity.

Though really, all that sharing and relating would only bring us closer. I can't do that. It wouldn't be fair to her to make her care for me, to put her life in danger that way. Any woman who makes the mistake of caring for me would end up paying for it in one way or another.

She seems good and frightened right now. That's for the best. If she's feeling intimidated, she's hating me and behaving herself. I can't ask for much more than that at the moment.

"I want you to think about what you need. For the wedding, all of it. I'm not in the mood to wander around from store to store while you make up your mind."

"I'm sure I won't need much," she whispers. I glance over to find her staring out the window, her folded hands pressed between her knees.

"You'll need a dress, at least."

She snorts. "Does it really matter?"

"I'm sure it will matter to your father and mother if you

show up for the wedding wearing sweatpants—or nothing but one of my dress shirts. Not exactly what they had in mind."

"Why do you even care?" An interesting question. I don't know how to answer it, so I let it go, and soon we fall back into uneasy silence.

That's a good thing. She needs to feel uneasy around me. We've drifted too far away from how things ought to be between us. I know it's up to me to change that.

I warn her again as we pull into a parking garage in town. "I'm serious. Do you doubt how bad I could make things for you if you decide to look for help while we're shopping?"

"I get it. I'll behave." A glance her way treats me to an eye roll.

I've never seen a woman look so unhappy about going shopping, but then I don't have much experience with this, either. I suppose my presence isn't helping things. It takes conscious effort to maintain a pleasant expression as I all but drag her down the street. "We'll go in here," I mutter, keeping a tight grip on her hand while gesturing toward a store with the other.

Her eyes widen. "Versace? Are you kidding?"

"Why would I kid?" She says nothing else, allowing me to lead her inside.

"This is nice," she whispers. I don't even know if she realized she said it, and I doubt she was talking to me. More like an inner thought she whispered without noticing.

And she's not wrong. The stores here in the Design District are top of the line, all the way, hence our being here. "What would you like?"

She blinks, her mouth falling open as we begin strolling through the place. "I have no idea."

"You need everything, don't you? Top to bottom."

"I guess, but..." She runs tentative fingers over a silk blouse, then winces when she looks at the price. "This is too nice for me."

Just when I think I have her figured out, she goes and says something like that. Too nice for her? Girls like her live along this strip, or at least that was the impression I got during prior visits. Even now, the street is crawling with girls her age carrying shopping bags over one arm and sipping smoothies and iced lattes.

"I would think it's fairly standard for a girl from your family."

She seems to shake herself out of it, then shrugs. "You're right. I... don't get a lot of opportunities to choose my own clothes."

That, I believe. "Well, if it would make you feel better, I can pick out things I like for you." I'm already looking around for a store clerk. "Remember. Not a word."

"I remember," she whispers a moment before a girl dressed in black from head to toe joins us, her brows lifted in anticipation. She's going to be glad she came to work today, at least if she works on commission.

"We have a lot of shopping to do," I explain, removing my sunglasses and hooking them over the neckline of my shirt. "And we might need your help carrying things and putting them aside until we're ready to check out."

The girl's mouth is practically watering. "Whatever you need, sir." She turns her gaze to Elena, wide-eyed and trembling a little. "Can I get you something to drink? Some cucumber water? Maybe a mimosa?"

"No, thank you," Elena whispers before I take her by the hand again and begin moving through the store with purpose. Jeans, blouses, T-shirts.

"You need underwear, don't you?" I murmur when the girl takes a stack of clothing to a dressing room for Elena to try it on.

"Of course." She eyes a table of lacy panties and thongs, and it's like pulling teeth to get her to pick any of them up.

"You could try enjoying yourself," I suggest in a soft growl. "I don't have to spend all this money on you."

"Then why are you?"

It occurs to me that this is the question that's kept her so quiet and so unwilling to participate. "You're going to be my wife, whether either of us likes it or not. You need clothes, and a man like me needs a wife who will look her best."

I can't tell her the entire reason. That if she doesn't start wearing something other than dress shirts with no pants, I can't guarantee how long I'll be able to control myself. Eventually, I'm going to do something I can't take back, like ravish her until she passes out, at the very least.

Eventually, she loosens up, at least offering opinions about the pieces I choose. "I think I prefer this one," she murmurs, choosing one pair of jeans over another.

"Fair enough. Please, decide what you want. I'm not cut out to be a personal shopper." That doesn't mean I'll give her a moment's peace—I tag along behind her, right on her heels all the way to the register, and again once we're in the Louis Vuitton store. I can tell by the way the women in the store smile and murmur to each other that I look like a caring, attentive boyfriend. Like I deserve an award for taking a woman to a store and doing something other than dragging my feet and rolling my eyes. In times like this, I realize how low the bar has been set for men in general. Days ago, I had this woman tied to a bed, where I threatened to take nude photos to send to her father. But I'm a prince for walking around a store with her.

There's one item we haven't searched for yet, and I can tell she wants to avoid it while we're wandering around Balenciaga. "We have to get you a dress for the wedding."

"Do we really? It feels so wrong."

"For fuck's sake. Does everything have to be an argument with you?" Truly, I doubt any man would want to marry her for any real, legitimate reason, not when she's so fucking impossible all the time. Everything has to be an argument.

"Here." I choose a white dress at random, one displayed on a mannequin. "That's your size, right? Go try this on."

"I don't—"

"You're going to try this on, or you're going to have a big problem. Now, which is it going to be?" When she only glares at me in defiance, I shrug before taking her hand. "So be it."

Before she can so much as take a breath, I drag her into the dressing room she's been using since we got here and follow her inside.

"You shouldn't do this," she whispers, but I'm oblivious to her bullshit at this point. I'm nowhere close to gentle as I all but tear off her clothes and toss them aside. I unzip the dress—she at least lifts her arms, so I can lower it over her head. It's sleeveless, with thin straps, in a soft fabric that flows around her as it cascades down her body, coming to a stop at her ankles.

"Turn," I choke out. My throat is so tight all of a sudden, along with my chest. I can hardly draw breath. She turns around, facing herself in the mirror while I zip up the back.

The word angel comes to mind. "You're beautiful," I murmur, hands on her shoulders as we both stare at her reflection. "You really are beautiful. I don't care if you want this dress or not. You have to wear it. It was made for you." It hugs her curves to perfection yet is modest enough for any parent to approve. It sets off her skin, her hair, and her eyes.

The word beautiful doesn't cover it. She's stunning, Elegant.

And so damn tempting, I don't know what to do. My hands tighten around her shoulders, and I turn her in place, taking her face in my hands. How am I supposed to resist her? How, when she is every beautiful, perfect thing rolled up into one alluring little package. Her eyes dart over my face, and she sinks her teeth into her lip, but she might as well be stroking my cock because that's how it feels; that's the electric jolt that runs through me at the sight of her hesitation.

I have no choice, do I? I have to do it. I have to taste her lips, have to lock myself with her even in this small way. I lower my head, brushing my tongue against her plump little mouth before claiming it with my own. She stiffens at first but only for a moment, only as long as it takes surprise to dissolve into something deeper, something that leaves her melting against me in an instant.

I stroke her soft cheeks with my thumbs before my hands slide lower, over her throat, her shoulders, down her arms, and back up until I'm cupping her tits through the dress. The material is thin enough that I feel her hard little nipples threatening to poke through, and the faintest brush of my thumbs over them leaves her whimpering, leaning in for more.

It's not enough. I need more, too, so much more. Visions swirl in my head, visions of pleasure, illicit and dangerous, visions of me pinning her against the wall and fucking her in this dress, popping her cherry with a hand over her mouth to stifle her cries.

"What are you doing?" she whispers when I push her up

against the wall before plunging my tongue deep inside her mouth again until she moans.

I love hearing her do that, no less than I love knowing I'm the one making her do it.

Her back hits the wall, and right away, I drop to my knees. She only puts up the faintest fight when I begin lifting the dress over my head.

"You shouldn't," she whispers.

If I wasn't so determined to taste her pussy, I might point out she hasn't said she doesn't want me to. It would be a lie if she did, anyway.

And sure enough, she's slick, practically dripping onto my tongue when I touch it to her sweet little lips. She gasps like I shocked her, her thighs already shaking, but that does nothing to stop me—on the contrary, it only makes me drive my tongue deep into her slit, lapping up every drop of her nectar.

"Oh, my god," she rasps, and I know if I were to look up at her, the sight would make me harder than I already am. All I can do is imagine pleasure washing over her face as I eat her with abandon, feasting on her, delighting in the strangled little whimpers she can't hold back. Knowing there are people outside the door, maybe in the room adjoining this one. I'm sure that must be going through her head, too, and all it makes me do is take her clit between my teeth and flick my tongue over the tip.

She stiffens, stops breathing, and a flood pours from her pulsing hole. One which I happily allow to coat my tongue, lips, and chin. Addictive, all-consuming. I'm going to need more of this, more of her.

And I'll have her once she puts this dress back on, and we say our vows.

The spark of anticipation the thought brings me is dangerous.

She's gasping for air once I stand and straighten the dress out. "Yes," I whisper, wiping my chin with the back of my hand. "This is the dress."

All she can do is nod, slumped against the wall, probably wondering what the hell just happened to her.

I'm wondering what's happened to me, too.

21

ALICIA

Well, at least the house doesn't feel so much like a tomb anymore. Now it's more like a train station, with people constantly walking in and out at all hours of the day. There are all kinds of deliveries coming in, too, and of course, I'm not allowed to know what any of them are.

Honestly, I don't care very much about that right now. I'm willing to accept having no say in anything that goes on in the house since it's not my house anyway. It's not like I want to be here. And I have no intention of staying for very long, either. This supposed wedding is coming up, but there's no way. There's just no way we're going through with it. I need to believe it's all nothing but a bunch of threats and empty promises.

At least I'm able to walk around the house again without being locked in here. I doubt that's any sort of kind gesture on Enzo's part. He's probably worried I'll start screaming and banging on the door and attract attention from deliverymen or whoever is always coming and going. I can't bring myself to care very much about his intentions. It means having a little bit of freedom, even if I still can't leave the house.

I have to wonder as I'm getting dressed if the whole point of taking me shopping was with this in mind. Did he know there were going to be more people coming to the house now? Probably. And his grandfather probably arranged the whole thing, too. So Enzo figured we should be prepared for company, meaning I had to wear something other than oversized dress shirts if I was going to be seen by anybody other than my supposed fiancé.

Now, I button a brand-new pair of jeans and an impossibly soft blouse that cost more than anything I've ever worn. I wonder how I'm supposed to eat in this thing without ruining it. How do rich people exist in the world with so many fine things that could easily be ruined?

That's an easy question to answer. They have enough money to buy more.

That's on my mind as I walk downstairs in hopes of making coffee and finding something for breakfast. I'm pretty sure I gave myself away a little bit while we were shopping—I caught him looking at me funny more than once and finally figured it was because I couldn't keep my mouth shut over how expensive everything was. I'm supposed to be from a powerful family, but I was acting like a poor girl. I need to inhabit this life I accidentally got myself into by pretending to be somebody I'm not. Which means walking around like I'm comfortable wearing an entire tuition payment like it's the kind of thing I do all the time.

Enzo's having a conversation with a pair of men in dark clothes, the three of them standing by the front door. He offers a distracted wave before going back to their huddle. Well, I guess it's better than him demanding to know what I'm doing walking around. He has to keep up appearances, too. The outside world isn't supposed to know I'm his prisoner.

There are a bunch of unmarked boxes by the front door, more deliveries. What the heck could it all be? What are they preparing for? It has to be for the wedding. A wedding I have no say over. No chance to do my own planning or anything like that.

But it's not a real wedding, and anyway, it's not going to happen. More than anything, I need to believe that. This is not actually going to happen.

Am I only fooling myself by thinking that way? My hands shake a little as I fix a pot of coffee, and I have to stop myself and take a few deep breaths to keep from panicking.

By the time the coffee finishes brewing, there's more noise than ever out in the living room. I look out to find an even larger cluster of men dressed in black coming in through the front door. What is this, some kind of convention? A bunch of undertakers getting together to talk about how sullen and creepy they all are? Because these are not friendly men—they're all scowling. A few of them glance my way with cold, hard eyes that make me shiver.

And then the crowd parts, and it's just Enzo and a man with a head of amazingly thick, silver hair. He's a proud man, with the bearing of somebody who's used to being in command. Even at his age and with all his wrinkles, he doesn't walk with that slightly stooped posture people his age normally develop. He keeps his square chin high, too, inspecting the many boxes waiting to be unpacked. So I was right. He has something to do with that.

He turns to Enzo and murmurs something. Enzo glances my way, our eyes locking for a second. I wish I could read his expression, but one thing is clear: the question was about me.

Nobody has to tell me who this man is. And frankly, I've wanted to set eyes on him. When he turns around and looks toward the kitchen, where I'm standing with a mug in my trembling hands, my skin crawls a little, and a wave of cold fear washes over me. Why do I get the feeling I just stepped into the snake pit?

He takes a step my way, and Enzo falls in step beside him, but the old man thrusts an arm out to stop his grandson from advancing. Oh God, help me. He wants us to have a little alone time. I wait for him, fear gnawing at me, twisting my stomach. I don't want him to see that, though something tells me he would anyway. Those dark eyes of his are much too shrewd to miss anything.

"So here she is," he says as he enters the room, offering a brittle smile that I guess is better than him being nasty or cruel.

"Hello. Here I am." What am I supposed to say? How am I supposed to behave in front of him? What's expected of me? Why is he even here? I guess he wanted to get a look at me before this supposed wedding of ours.

He takes a seat at the kitchen table, and two guards hover behind him. Nobody has to tell me that's their job. They might as well have it tattooed on their foreheads, burly men who'd look more at home in a wrestling ring or guarding the front door of a bar or club.

What am I supposed to do? There's an expectant sort of energy in the air like he's waiting for me to make a move. I wish somebody had told me the rules of this game in advance.

"Can I get you some coffee?" I offer, for lack of anything better to say.

He scoffs, and right there, I see the influence he's had on Enzo. I wonder how many times he's watched his grandfather do that, but it's been so frequent that he picked up the habit himself. "Coffee? I need a little something stronger than that. Two fingers of whiskey on the rocks."

It's a little earlier in the day than I would have my first drink, but I guess a man of his age has every right to decide for himself. I go over to the bar cart, glancing in Enzo's direction when I do. He's talking with more men, his body half turned in my direction. Like his attention is split, though he doesn't want to show it. There's no way he can be as anxious about this as I am, is there? I wonder why.

I pour the drink, adding ice cubes from the little bucket on the cart, then take the glass to the table. "Here you are, sir."

"Thank you. Please, have a seat. I've been anxious to get to know you better."

Yes, I just bet he has. There's an almost playful tone in his voice, like this is all a big joke—but it's more like the way a bully would laugh as he pins down his target. At least that's how it sounds to me right now when I'm trying so hard not to shake. What happens if I mess up, and he figures out this has all been a big lie?

I lower myself into a chair at his right hand while he savors the first sip of whiskey. "I never was much of a coffee drinker," he explains, rattling the ice in the glass. "Nowadays, my doctor would rather I avoid it. Blood pressure, and all that." I nod for lack of anything better to do. His doctor is more than likely right. The man has to be at least seventy years old.

"Tell me about yourself," he continues, eyeing me while wearing an expression I can't read.

"What would you like to know?" Oh, this is bad. This is so bad. I don't know what I'm supposed to say. I don't even know who I'm supposed to be.

"Are you generally in good health?"

A strange way to lead off, but at least I can answer this one without having to make anything up. "Yes, I always have been."

"No serious illnesses?"

"Not really. The normal colds, that sort of thing. An ear infection or two when I was younger."

"And what about your reproductive system? Is everything in order there?"

Surprise widens my eyes for a second, but I manage to keep a handle on myself. "As far as I know."

"Everything working normally?"

"Yes, always." My skin's crawling, and I want more than anything to be out of this room, away from this man with his intrusive questions. Next thing I know, he'll point me to a table with stirrups set up at the end. Maybe the whole setup is waiting in one of those boxes.

He folds his arms on the table, leaning a little closer. But there's no intimacy in the gesture. It's not like we're two people having a private and slightly uncomfortable conversation, so he wants to make it easier on me. No, he's closing in on his prey, is all. He can pretend all he wants, but I see right through him—and it's terrifying. "Tell me about your family."

Fear skitters down my spine, and I'm afraid I'm going to scream. My heart's pounding against my ribs, and my throat tightens until I know I won't be able to get a word out. A sip of coffee helps loosen me up a little. "What would you like to know?" I manage to whisper. *Oh please, God. Don't let him be what ends me.* As much as I would rather cut off an arm than marry Enzo, I don't need to lose my life over this.

"Have you any siblings?"

I don't know what the correct answer is because I don't know who they think I am. What if I say the wrong thing, and he knows right away that I'm lying? All I can do is tell the truth, I guess. "No. I was an only child."

"And why is that?" When I frown in confusion, he clarifies. "Was your mother unable to have any more?"

"I really don't know. I guess it just never happened for them."

"Are your parents healthy?"

"As far as I know, yes. I don't know of any history of illness in my family on either side."

"And your parents, how many siblings do they have?"

I'm so damn confused. What is the point of all of this? Should I have brought a family album along with me before essentially being kidnapped? "Um, my father has two sisters, and my mom has one of each."

"Not exactly a large family, but respectable."

I shrug because what am I supposed to say? I don't even know if what I told him matches up to the girl he thinks I am.

He looks me up and down without bothering to hide it. "You look healthy enough. And you're a pleasure to look at, if you'll permit an old man to reflect on what he'd do if he was a few decades younger." My cheeks go warm, and I duck my head, both slightly flattered and a lot more disgusted. "You'll make beautiful babies with my grandson. They will certainly be blessed genetically."

That's all this is about. Wanting children to grow the family. That's what all these questions have been leading to. He wants to make sure I can give him lots of great-grandchildren. I don't know if that's sort of sweet or completely disgusting, considering the family he wants me to build. A bunch of little Enzo clones? No fucking chance. I would never raise a child the way he raised his grandson. I would want my children to have a chance in life of being actual, decent people. Not some twisted, haunted shells.

I realize he's waiting for me to say something. How am I supposed to respond to that? "I'm glad you approve."

His thin mouth stretches in a smile that goes at least part way toward making him seem more human and approachable. But I'm not fooling myself. This isn't some kindly old man. He's a viper if ever I saw one, and anybody stupid enough to underestimate him because of his age would deserve whatever they got.

He even goes so far as to pat my hand, his skin thin and almost papery. "Your marriage to my Enzo is going to cement a great deal between our families," he predicts, still smiling.

And just as suddenly as a snake striking, his hand tightens around my wrist until pain races up my arm. "But if you don't get pregnant quickly," he continues, his voice lower now, "I will kill you myself and send your body to your father. No more deal."

I can't say anything. I'm sure he doesn't even want me to respond. I'm too shocked to do anything but sit still, trembling despite my best efforts to hide it, while he gestures to his guards before standing and leaving the room without another word.

I have to get pregnant, or he's going to kill me. I just met the man, but I know in my heart that was not an idle threat.

22

ENZO

What a fucking day. Between my grandfather coming over and all the deliveries for the wedding, I'm beyond exhausted by the time all is said and done. It's well past eight o'clock by the time the townhouse empties out, leaving just Elena and me. I never knew getting married would end up being such a headache, but of course, this situation is more fraught with tension than it might be otherwise. Namely, because I don't trust Alvarez as far as I can throw him. We've made arrangements for men to guard the house, the backyard where the ceremony will take place, all of it. Alvarez will have men of his own, so we've agreed on how many armed bodyguards both families can use on the day of the ceremony.

Three days. Three days from now. It's probably for the best that the ceremony will take place so soon. Less time for second-guessing everything, less time for regret. No, I can spend the rest of my life regretting the decisions I've made. Lucky me.

Now, all I want is a little peace and quiet as I step into the house after having gone over arrangements yet another time, in this case, with the minister charged with performing the ceremony. I tuck my phone into my pocket and notice for the first time the way my stomach is growling. The kitchen is dark, the stove cold. It doesn't look like Elena fixed herself any dinner. It might not be a bad idea to order something in and sit down together and catch her up on some of the arrangements we made today. Not that it matters one way or another—she has no say in any of this, something I'm sure she's aware of by now—but it feels like I should at least inform her of what she's in for on our so-called big day.

I almost hate who she's turning me into. Since when am I considerate? Life is much easier when I'm the only person I'm concerned with.

It surprises me to find her on the sofa, curled in a ball, holding a pillow to her chest. She never turned on a light and is now lying in darkness.

And she's crying.

I'm torn. Crying has never been something I've dealt well with, no matter who's doing it. Emotions, in general, are not my forte. I don't feel like sitting around and watching her drip snot all over everything, and God forbid she wants me to hold her or something awkward like that.

At the same time, the little sounds she makes remind me of a wounded animal. I might be a monster, but a wounded animal is not something I can simply pass by and pretend I didn't notice.

"What's wrong?"

She jumps like she truly didn't realize I was standing here, not ten feet from where she's weeping. "Don't worry about it. I'll be fine. I should have gone upstairs or something so you wouldn't have to worry about me."

I don't know if she means it or if she's only looking for sympathy. "It's a little late for that now, isn't it?" I take a seat on the coffee table, facing her. "What's happening? Nervous about the wedding?"

"No. I mean, yes, of course I am. This is all happening so fast, like I'm on a train and can't control the speed. I'm afraid it's going to derail."

She has a talent for metaphors. "I can relate to that. I'm having a hard time coming to terms with this schedule myself. But you knew it was going to be happening very soon. Is it just hitting you now?"

She's quiet for so long that if I didn't know better, I'd think she fell asleep. When an eternity passes, and she still doesn't answer, I get up and turn the light on.

"No, I don't want you to see me." She buries her face in the pillow as if that makes a difference.

"Out with it. I'm not going to have you lying around crying until the wedding." When she still doesn't answer, I add, "In case you couldn't tell, this is me trying to be nice. It's not something that happens often."

She sighs heavily but finally lifts her face from the pillow. Her eyes are red-rimmed and swollen, her cheeks soaked with tears. "I keep telling myself to get over it, but... he really scared me."

"Who did?"

She looks guilty and regretful. "Promise you won't get mad."

"Out with it," I said.

In a tiny voice, she whispers, "Your grandfather."

Son of a bitch. I should have known. He wanted to speak to her alone, without me being around. I knew he would more than likely try to scare her a little, try to make sure she's frightened into behaving herself and being the respectful little wife he wants for me.

"I know better than to ask for forgiveness on another person's behalf," I murmur. "But that's just how he is. As soon as he thought I was old enough to find a wife, he made it his life's mission to marry me off. Honestly, if it were anyone else, it would be funny. Like something out of a movie or a TV show. The meddling grandfather determined to find a wife for his grandson before he dies."

"That's not it."

"Then what is it?"

She runs the heel of her hand under both eyes and shakes her head. "You know what? Ask him yourself. I want you to hear what he said. If he even tells you the truth."

"I'll call him," I offer, then try to change the subject. "Are you hungry? I could order dinner."

"I don't have an appetite. I just want to sleep." She sits up, her chin still quivering in spite of the sudden about-face she's taken. "I'm going to go up to my room."

It's not a question. She isn't asking for permission. I sit, helpless and concerned, while she climbs the stairs one slow tread at a time.

It's foreign, the indignation that flares to life as I reach for my phone. The indignation itself isn't the problem—the man has given me more than enough reason over the years to be indignant, even to resent him.

But now he's fucking with her, the woman who's supposed to be my wife in a matter of days. She's going to be mine, which means she's not his to screw around with. I highly doubt he'll enjoy hearing that, but that's not going to stop me. He's the one so concerned with making sure this wedding goes off without a hitch. Why would he throw a wrench into the plans?

The moment he answers, I jump on him before he has the chance to do the same to me. "What did you say to her?"

Grandfather sputters, "What are you referring to?"

"No. Do me the favor of not pulling the doddering old man bullshit act on me. You forget I've watched you do it before. I know exactly how it goes."

"Have you forgotten who you're speaking to?"

"At least you sound more like yourself now." I look up the stairs. "What did you say to Elena? And please, don't lie."

"We had a lovely discussion. She's a fine girl, respectful toward her elders and eager to please. I couldn't be more approving."

My patience, which is already paper-thin, is starting to dwindle. "So why don't you try telling me why I found her drowning in tears just now?"

He scoffs, and it's easy to imagine him sitting back with a cigar and a glass of whiskey, both against the doctor's orders. "You know how women are. I'm sure the excitement from planning the wedding and knowing she'll be your wife within a few days' time has taken its toll."

Another response that isn't the one I want. "Grandfather. This is me you're talking to. She spoke specifically of you, of something you said to her. Now I want you to tell me what it was. Please, at least give me the courtesy of being upfront."

"I wished her happiness, and that I hope the two of you make a lot of babies. They'll be beautiful—that much, I know I said. Between the two of you, there's no chance of your children being anything but cherubs."

"I'm sure she felt pressured by that." I also don't believe him. I doubt she's in any hurry to bear my children, but why would she be a sobbing wreck as a result of something as innocent as what he just described?

"Pardon me, but I don't care very much either way whether or not she feels pressured. And frankly, she'd better get used to pressure if she's going to be any sort of wife to you. You know this."

"At the moment, it doesn't matter what I know. It matters that she's hysterical and in pain. You're the one forcing me into this arrangement. Is it so beyond the pale that I would care whether the woman I'm being forced to marry is sobbing her heart out over something you said to her?"

"I must say," he gloats, "I approve of the way you've taken this protective stance. It bodes well for your future with her."

The man missed his calling. He should have studied tap dance since he's already so skilled at dancing around any topic he doesn't wish to discuss. "This is difficult enough," I grumble. "I don't need you making it more difficult for me. Forgive me if that's disrespectful, but that's the situation."

"Let's face facts. The reality of the situation is quite clear. You're going to need to impregnate that girl, and soon. The only way to cement this arrangement is if she's carrying your child."

I could get whiplash from a single conversation with this man. "Hold on. One thing at a time, please. I've barely wrapped my head around the wedding—"

"You aren't listening," he barks. "You will get that girl pregnant, and you will do it immediately. I don't care what it takes. I don't care if you are fucking her morning, noon, and night. I don't care if the ceremony is delayed because you're busy defiling that girl. You're going to do this, end of story."

"Do I have a deadline?" I ask, snickering.

"Preferably, I would like her to be pregnant by the time she walks down the aisle."

A laugh bursts out of me before I know what's happening. When he doesn't laugh along with me, my mouth falls open in shock. "Grandfather, I realize we've never had any in-depth talks about the so-called birds and bees, but I assume you understand how these things work."

"Meaning?"

"Meaning it doesn't work that way. We're getting married in three days. Even if she was at that point in her cycle, there's not a test on earth that would be able to pick up something like that if I slept with her tonight."

"Do you think I care about the specifics? She will walk down that aisle with your seed inside her, or else."

"And exactly how would anyone know whether or not she did? Are we going to have one of those medieval rituals where a doctor comes in and examines her? Or would you prefer to do it yourself?"

"Watch it, boy," he warns.

"Forgive me, but this is veering into bizarre territory. I understand the need to further the family line, but what you're asking for is medically impossible."

"It's medically impossible for you to fuck that girl?"

"No, of course not."

"There you are. Do it. More than once. You have to make a convincing show of this, or else Alvarez might call the whole thing off at the last moment. We can't have that."

This is becoming more twisted by the moment. "Am I supposed to announce to him that I deflowered his daughter, and she'll be ruined if she ends up pregnant with my baby? Maybe he'll challenge me to a duel over it. You'll have to bring the pistols."

"I'm glad you find this amusing."

"I have never been less amused in my life."

"If Josef Alvarez calls off this wedding, and you didn't do everything within your power to make certain it doesn't happen, you'll be far less amused than you are now. Mark my words. Have I ever made an empty threat?"

"No," I mutter. He's caught me again. He's always got me. No matter how old I get, no matter how experienced, none of it matters. He's always at least one step ahead.

"You're damn right I haven't. Get off the phone with me and get inside that girl. I'm sure you won't have any trouble with that—she's a nice little piece of ass. You could have done much worse if you had to kidnap a girl."

Even by my standards, it seems sick to accept praise for something like that, so I don't bother thanking him.

"I'd better go. I have work to do." It's an excuse to get off the phone. I'm not sure how much longer I can be civil.

I have to do this. There's no question in my mind. I have to at least make an effort.

And while I can't exactly say the idea of fucking her is a hardship, the idea of hurting her in the process is another story.

BEAST

23
ALICIA

Something's up.

I feel it in the air, the way something has changed. It's not so much in anything specific Enzo says or does. It's more the general feeling. He's paying more attention to me today than he normally does, but not in an angry, *you're my prisoner, so you have to do as I say* kind of way. I got enough of that before to recognize it.

No, now it's like he's actually paying attention to me as a person, ever since yesterday, with that disastrous meeting with his grandfather. It seemed like he really cared that I was upset after all was said and done. And I'm sure more than a little bit of that has to do with the fact that this is his life, too. He's finally starting to clue in to the fact that we're in this together. I'm just as trapped as he is, and neither of us has to like it.

After dinner—a meal we shared together in the kitchen after he asked what kind of food I would like to order in—he makes a strange suggestion. "Why don't you go up and take a shower? I have a little surprise for you."

I sit and wait for the punchline, but there isn't one. "Like, a good surprise?"

He snorts, then nods. "I think so."

"You're going to make me wait, aren't you?"

He lifts a shoulder, and his mouth tugs up at the corner. "The sooner you get in the shower, the sooner you'll find out what it is. It's really up to you."

Yes, something is definitely up. He's almost cheerful and upbeat. In other words, the exact opposite of who he's been from the beginning of this mess. What's he going to do? Take me to his grandfather's, so I can go through an invasive physical exam? Or maybe this is some sick, twisted lead-up to me finding out they know I've been lying this whole time. I've seen *The Godfather*. I know how things like this work.

As I climb the stairs because I don't have a choice, I can't shake the memory of Michael's traitorous brother-in-law thinking he's on his way to the airport when really, someone's lying in wait for him in the car. And up until the very last moment, everyone lied to his face to make him think he was safe.

No, Enzo wouldn't do that to me. Not that I have any ideas about him caring. I'm not that far gone. But he's got a lot riding on this marriage arrangement, too. I don't doubt his grandfather gave him pretty much the same ultimatum he gave me. This twisted obsession with making sure we have a baby. It's so gross.

I try to remind myself as I'm washing up that it's in Enzo's best interests to protect me now. It helps me shake off the worst of my apprehension.

Not all of it. I'm still trembling and hesitant once I finish drying off, stepping out of the bathroom with the towel wrapped around me. My bedroom door is open, the light on.

My feet are like lead as I drag myself down the hall, forcing myself to face whatever is coming.

"There you are. That was fast, actually. I just finished laying these things out for you." He sweeps an arm over the bed, gesturing to an outfit that wasn't there before I got in the shower.

It's not the outfit that catches my attention and holds it. It's him. In the time it took me to shower, he changed into a sexy black suit with a white shirt, with the collar unbuttoned to reveal a hint of his broad, tanned chest. He looks like a million bucks, and it's enough to take my breath away at first.

I realize he's staring at me, waiting for me to say something while I wrestle with my hormones. "What's this all about?" I finally murmur, prying my eyes from him so I can check out what he left for me.

"I was thinking. Here we are, on the verge of getting married, but we've never even gone on a date. That doesn't seem right, does it?"

That doesn't seem right? Out of everything that's happened since he discovered me in that warehouse, what's bothering him is the fact that we've never been on a date before we were forced into marriage?

"Wow, this is really nice." I run the backs of my fingers along the blood-red satin dress. It's stunning, really. I wonder how he got his hands on it—it's not one of the things he bought me when we went shopping.

"Go ahead, get yourself ready." He's out of the room before I can think to ask exactly where we're going. I doubt it would matter if I asked, anyway. It's not like I have any say in this.

Besides, it might not be so bad. A night out means a night away from the house, at least. And I'm sure that once he's out in public around other people and has to behave himself, he could probably be pretty charming.

And if we are relating to each other one-on-one, just two people stuck in an impossible situation, he might feel a little more sympathy for me. It can't hurt to try to win him over a little, can it?

Something tells me I'm going to win him over, at least when it comes to how I look. The dress fits like a glove like it was made just for me. It hugs my curves, coming to a stop an inch above my knee and low cut enough that my boobs look like they want to spill out of it. But the dress is constructed well enough that it's only an illusion. I can't help but like what I see when I check myself out in the full-length bathroom mirror once I've finished applying some of the makeup I snagged during our shopping trip. I'm glad I thought about that. No girl can get married without at least a little bit of makeup, I told him. Now I don't have to go out barefaced, feeling sloppy.

Even as I offer myself a tiny smile in the mirror once I'm finished checking myself out, something keeps tugging at my heart, making it impossible to feel confident. I finally realize what it is while slipping on a pair of black heels: the last time I got dressed up like this, I was getting ready to go to the warehouse.

A chill runs through me, finally settling in my stomach in the form of a block of ice. At least, that's what it feels like. How is it possible my life has changed so much in such a short amount of time? Will I ever be able to go back to the way it used to be? I'm not sure how I could. I'm a different person now; at least, that's how it feels. I've been through situations I never imagined before. I'm not the Alicia I used to be, and I never will be again. It's enough to make frustrated tears threaten to well up in my eyes, but I'm determined to blink them back. Not only because I don't want to give in to despair—I'm afraid I'd never find my way out—but I just finished my makeup and don't want to keep Enzo waiting. If he's in a good mood, he's not being cruel and abusive.

Once I'm satisfied, I take the stairs slowly, careful in my new stilettos. He's waiting in the living room, sipping a glass of whiskey while checking something on his phone. The sound of my footfalls on the stairs makes him glance up, distracted, before he does a complete double take. His mouth falls open slightly, and his eyes follow my every move.

In other words, I think I'm making a good impression.

"How do I look?" I hold my arms out to the sides and do a slow turn. I'm pretty sure he hasn't breathed since he caught sight of me.

"You look... fucking hot."

I burst out laughing before I can help myself. "Thank you. So do you, by the way." Does he ever. And he smells even better, his musky cologne leaving me fighting the urge to lean in and breathe deep.

"All a guy has to do is put on a suit."

"Yeah, and that's really unfair." We share an awkward little grin before I ask, "So where are we going?"

"I thought we'd stop in at a club my family owns. It's a little place, nothing over the top or anything like that. I figured we could do a little dancing, have some drinks, just hang out together for a while."

I hope he's not serious about the dancing part because I am no one's idea of graceful or even particularly coordinated. But I'm not about to protest, either. A night out? The closest I've come to normalcy since I got in the Uber to go to the warehouse? Yeah. I think that sounds like a good idea.

This time, he's not driving, so he opens the back door to a sleek black car before helping me in, then walks around to the other side so he can slide in beside me. God, he is overwhelming and too gorgeous for my own good. Some people can pull off that effortlessly sexy look he's got going on right now. All I know is that when his eyes meet mine as the car begins rolling down the driveway, his grandfather would be thrilled because I'm pretty sure I got pregnant without him putting a hand on me.

He was right about the club, which I'm glad to see is more of an intimate bar with a dance floor. There are still plenty of people around, a few dozen dancers on the floor with another group clustered around the bar, but at least I won't have to scream to be heard.

"Do you come here a lot?" I ask as he ushers me through the crowd with a hand against my lower back. I'd swear he's burning my skin through the dress. *Focus, girl. Don't let your horniness get in the way.*

"From time to time. I don't have much of a social life." Right, but that doesn't stop just about everybody who sees him from taking a step back or nodding in recognition. Is it respect or fear? Is there a difference in this world?

"Always busy with work?"

"Something like that." We reach the bar, where a trio of guys take an interest in me, at least if the way they stare at me means anything. Enzo very deliberately positions himself between them and me, turning his back to them like they don't mean anything. Does he even know how possessive he's acting right now?

Dammit, and I want to read into it, don't I? I hope this night doesn't end up turning into a mistake.

I ask for a glass of white wine while Enzo orders whiskey

for himself. "What about you?" he asks once we have our drinks, which seem to appear out of thin air like the bartender was waiting for us. The perks of being related to the owner, I guess.

"What about me?"

He waves a hand, indicating everything around us. "Do you go out a lot?"

"I can probably count on one hand the number of times I've been to a club, any club."

"Really?" He tips his head to the side, frowning like he's puzzled by this.

"Is that such a big surprise?"

"I don't know. I figured you're young, you were in school. Isn't that what people do in college?"

"Maybe some people. It never interested me much." I have to bite my tongue before I slip up and explain I never exactly had the money for a social life. It would be so easy to trip up and say the wrong thing—and dammit, the wine I'm holding probably isn't going to make it any easier to guard the things I say. I didn't think about that. I'm going to have to take it easy on the booze.

"I'm more of a homebody," I conclude with a shrug. "I've always been that way."

"That's not a bad thing." Yes, I'm sure the idea of him having a quiet little homebody for a wife, somebody who he won't have to worry about, is a big relief.

Once our glasses are empty, he grins. "Come on." He winds his fingers around mine and begins pulling me away from the bar toward the floor. "I want to see the way you move in that dress."

Okay, that is super hot, but still. "I'm not much of a dancer. I have to tell you that right now."

"Don't worry about it. Just relax, and have a little fun. It doesn't matter if you're any good or not." Easy for him to say. I've never stepped on his foot, but I'm probably going to by the time we're finished.

Once we reach the center of the floor, the song changes to something with a driving, Latin beat. He grins like this is exactly what he wanted to hear as he turns to me, placing his hands on my waist. "Just move with me," he calls out over the music. "That's all you have to do. Relax, and let me lead you around."

I'm still way too nervous, but what the hell? What's the worst that could happen? Maybe I shouldn't ask myself that question.

Once he starts moving, though, my apprehension dissolves. I thought he was sexy before? The man swivels his hips, drawing me close before taking my right hand in his left and pressing his right hand against my back. "Just follow my lead," he reminds me with a wink before moving again, his body brushing against mine with every swivel of his hips, every twist of his waist. I could happily stand here and watch him move all day, but instead, I have the joy of trying to keep up.

He laughs indulgently when I stumble a little, then catches me and holds me in place before I can fall over. "Relax," he implores. "You're in safe hands. Feel the music. Don't think about it. Just go with it."

When he flashes a sexy grin, I can't help but think he could talk me into just about anything if he tried.

Red warning flags wave like crazy in my head, but what am I supposed to do? I don't have a choice but to go with it like he says. Before long, I can almost imagine I'm not a bad dancer myself. The deeper I sink into the music, the easier it is to let go of my inhibitions and let my body flow the way he does with his. Once I stop thinking and analyzing everything, it's possible to simply respond to the rhythm and to how shockingly hot it is for us to be this close, moving in sync like we are. He leans in until our cheeks touch, his breath hot on my neck and shoulder. So why do I shiver if all he's doing is heating me?

Dear Lord, am I in trouble.

So much trouble, in fact, that when he suggests getting another drink, I agree without thinking about it. Wasn't I just telling myself I had to be careful? What am I trying to do, sabotage myself?

The fact is, even in my slightly buzzed and extremely horny state, I still understand I just want to have fun. For a little while, all I want is to pretend this is normal. We're just two people who have a crazy kind of chemistry, enjoying each other, flirting a little, standing way too close to each other as we sip our drinks. His hand grazes my back before dipping a little lower and sweeping over the curve of my ass. My legs just about buckle while wetness pools in my panties. He could touch my pussy once right now, and I'd probably burst into flames.

And I think he knows that since he caresses my ass again. "It was made for you," he informs me in a low growl, making me shiver while my nipples harden almost painfully. "But it would look better on my bedroom floor."

Yes, he knows he has me where he wants me. Just like he knows that once we get back to the house, there's no way I could resist being pulled into his bedroom.

The fact is, I hardly try.

BEAST

24

ENZO

I wish I could go into this wholeheartedly. I wish I didn't feel conflicted about pulling her into my room and ending the night the way it was always meant to end. Whether she knows it or not, this was the plan from the moment I announced we were going out. Will she ever put it together? I don't know. In spite of everything she's been through and everything I'm sure she's seen from the world around her—the world we both inhabit—she still let me lead her into this. She offered not a single moment of hesitation.

Just like she's not hesitating now when I take her in my arms, pressing my body to hers and grinding my growing cock against her. "All night, this is all I could think of doing," I murmur before touching my lips to her throat. She sighs, and the sound goes right through me like a shock wave, so sudden and unexpected. My arms clench around her, and I have to stop myself from throwing her on the bed and ending this entire evening sooner than I'd planned.

I want her to want this, to want it with every ounce and every fiber of her being. I want her completely wrapped up in me, in the moment, in anticipation of what's to come. I want her to lose herself in me.

I don't want her to regret it. That's the least I can do. I might have no choice but to seduce her tonight, but I can make sure she's fully ready and fully with me.

And so I take my time rather than throwing her to the bed and fucking her senseless. I take a slow tour of her body, my hands sliding along her back, gently caressing the curve of her ass. She shudders slightly, gasping in surprise. Like she's never felt this way before, and I doubt she has. Nothing I've shown her so far comes close to what she's about to experience. What I'm going to make sure she experiences.

By the time I've finished touching her, she's shaking, weak to the point where I'm almost holding her up. That's the sign I'm looking for. The next step is slowly unzipping her dress, an inch at a time. My anticipation is growing just like hers is, my own zipper about ready to break from the strain of my eager, rigid cock. I allow my fingertips to glide over every bit of skin I expose as I work the zipper lower until, finally, it can't go any farther, and I have the pleasure of peeling the dress away from her, of listening as her breath gets shorter and sharper. Much more of this, and she'll collapse.

"Why don't you sit down?" I whisper in her ear before running my tongue over the lobe and making her shudder and moan. Once the dress is in a puddle around her ankles, she steps out of it, leaving her in nothing more than lacy panties and a bra I remember buying for her at the store. At the time, I couldn't have imagined how her generous breasts would fill the cups, almost spilling over, begging for me to bury my face between them. Or to slide my cock back and forth while she holds out her tongue to lick me.

Slow down. If I keep thinking along those lines, I'll end up coming in my pants.

Instead of indulging myself in her lusciousness, I take a step back before I begin the process of removing my own clothes. Her chest heaves with every ragged breath, and unless my eyes deceive me, she's rubbing her thighs together. Is she aware of it? Or is her body merely fighting for a measure of relief?

I hold her gaze as I remove my jacket and lay it across the foot of the bed. Then I slowly work my shirt out from the waistband of my slacks and begin unbuttoning it—slowly, so slowly, teasing her, building her anticipation with every button I pop. She's seen me naked before, but this is different, and I know it is. Because now she's looking at me through the haze of lust. Now she's anticipating my body on top of hers, against hers.

Finally, I remove the shirt and kick off my shoes before loosening my belt. She breaks eye contact in favor of staring down at the bulge so very obviously jutting its way out in front of me. Her interest only makes me move slower, even though it's killing me. Let her wait. Let her imagine what my erect cock looks like and how I'll wreck her with it once I'm inside her. I unbutton the waist, then unzip, allowing the pants to fall so only my boxers stand in the way.

She bites her lip when I run my palm over my covered length, her throat working when she swallows what's pooling in her mouth. A mouth I can't wait to fuck, to fill. There's a wet spot on the front of my underwear by the time I take the waistband and lower them, springing free for her inspection. Her eyes widen, her nostrils flare, and I can smell her arousal in the air. That sweet, musky scent drawing me in as she drips with excitement. I've tasted her already, and I haven't been able to forget her unique flavor, one which I now need to coat my tongue.

And so I step up in front of her and gently but firmly lower her to the bed until she is on her back, her feet on the floor. Her short, ragged breaths convey both her excitement and her nervousness. "Don't worry," I whisper, running my lips over her inner thighs until she squirms. "By the time I'm finished, you'll be begging me to fuck you. But first, I want to make sure you're ready."

I pull away the panties blocking my view of her slick lips, gratified to find her sopping wet, her moisture having soaked into the lacy fabric. I hold it to my nose and inhale deeply, aware of the fact she's watching. She sighs softly, sweetly, but there's something under it I can't ignore. Hunger. Need.

A need I'm going to happily fill. I take her feet and place them on my shoulders, then nudge her thighs farther apart until her knees fall to the sides and bare all of her to me.

"So pretty," I whisper, running a thumb along her slit, watching in fascination as even more glistening juice drips from her. I catch it on my thumb, then raise it to my lips, sucking it clean. All that does is add fuel to the fire. It's not enough. I doubt it ever will be.

But I tease her some more, and myself in the process, by trailing my tongue along the outside of her lips, in the incredibly smooth crease between them and her thighs. She bucks and writhes, moaning helplessly, gripping the sheets in both hands and twisting them. Her heels dig into my shoulders, and I welcome the pressure, knowing everything I do now will only pay off when she unravels around me. And all the while, I inhale her scent, allowing it to drive me wild just as I'm driving her wild.

And when I finally trace her shining slit with my tongue,

her sharp gasp makes precum drip from my tip. She's on fire, already close to exploding, but I ease my way into it, though it would be so easy to make her come until her eyes rolled back right this very moment. No. Instead, I lick her slowly, deliberately, drawing one moan after another from deep in her chest, seemingly from down in her toes. Animal grunts, sounds I've never heard from her before. Or from any woman, for that matter. And I haven't yet dipped deeper, haven't breached her lips to reach her shining, pink flesh.

When I do, she lifts her hips, using her feet on my shoulders as leverage, and begins riding my face. I wasn't expecting this, and it's so fucking hot that I have to take hold of myself and stroke slowly because, god, the anticipation is killing me. I'm so hard, it hurts, and my swollen balls are aching to be emptied.

To be emptied into her. A pang of regret lances through me, but I push it aside in favor of working her clit with the slightest, lightest feather touch.

It turns out there's only so much I can control here. Her body is a wire already tightened to the point where it's ready to snap. It takes nothing to push her over the edge, and she falls over with a soft scream while her pussy twitches in time with every rapid beat of her heart. And every pulse sends fresh juice my way. I catch every drop, savoring her as my own excitement grows.

"Oh my god," she whispers, her voice thick.

She wants to see God? I think I can arrange for that. Yet when I stand, prepared to work my way into her, she sits up.

"Can I do that for you?" The uncertainty in the question touches something deep inside me. She's so innocent, unworldly, and eager to please.

And it's yet another good sign, telling me I'm on the right

track here. "If you're sure," I murmur, stroking myself in front of her face. She looks overwhelmed but also eager. "Here. Touch it."

She closes her fingers around my shaft, and I close my eyes in response, thrilled even at her inexperienced touch. She mimics the way I stroked myself, twisting her hand slightly when she reaches the head.

"That's good," I murmur, stroking her hair. "Now, use your tongue. Go ahead. Don't be scared—I'll tell you what to do."

"I've seen some of this before," she whispers, and I could almost laugh at her innocence.

"Watching porn?" I tease, chuckling at the way she blushes. "Here's a hint: bobbing up and down in a blur isn't always the best way to go. You want to start out slow. And when the time comes, I'll set the pace. Okay?"

She nods before touching her tongue to my head. I suck in a gasp, my teeth clenched, but I nod when she looks up at me. "That's nice. Do that again." And she does, then again, licking like she's tasting a lollipop.

"Now, put it in your mouth. You don't have to suck hard. Just apply a little pressure." It's so easy to get her to do what I want. She's so determined to please me the way I've pleased her. It's heady, powerful, and dangerous. I could get used to this. And I suppose I'll have to.

What I don't need is the feelings she stirs in me. How touched I am by her on a level much deeper than the physical. How proud I am of how she tries to take all of me at once, lowering her head until she gags. I only stroke her hair again, then take a handful and tug lightly.

"Let me," I grunt, nearing the end of my control already. "Just hold steady."

And then I move, thrusting my hips, fucking her face

slowly at first, gently. But that's not enough for long, especially when she lifts her eyes and meets mine, and the intensity of our connection deepens. Soon she is whimpering in surprise and confusion, but I don't care. I want to do this. I need to do this. Even when her eyes water, threatening tears, it only makes me want to take her harder.

The threat of coming down her throat makes me pull out. She wipes her mouth with the back of her hand, breathing hard. But there's something in her eyes that wasn't there before. Satisfaction? Maybe a sense of pride? I'm not deluded —I don't think sucking my cock actually made her proud— but maybe it's the fact that she took it so well.

"Lie back again," I whisper, and this time I follow her, lowering myself until my body is draped over hers. Even though it's clear she thinks I'm going to enter her now, I don't, choosing instead to play with her again. With her tits, the sensitive skin of her throat, her thighs, her ass. I explore every inch of her, even her ankles and the soles of her feet, touching her until she groans in frustration every time I come close to her pussy without making contact.

"Please..." she whispers, her eyes squeezed shut, her face flushed, screwed up in concentration.

"Please, what?"

"Please, take me." She pulls me closer. "Please, Enzo."

Fuck, how could any man resist this? I know I'm not strong enough and don't want to be. I want to give in to what I've wanted ever since I set eyes on her. To claim her, own her, make her scream my name.

She's certainly wet enough to make it easy on her, the wet spot under her ass bringing me a measure of gladness as I move between her legs. I don't want this to hurt her. She'll hurt enough if and when she finds out this was all planned. And not even by me. I didn't want to do this to her as much as my body craves her. It still doesn't seem fair.

But neither does letting this pussy go unclaimed, and my dripping cock is so close to her pulsing hole. "I'll take it slow at first," I promise, and all she does in response is dig her nails into my ass and pull me closer. There's no question of what she wants. She doesn't even ask me about condoms. Good thing because I would have to make up an excuse if she did.

This is what he wants? This is what he'll get. But I can't pretend I won't enjoy it.

I drag the swollen head of my cock through her folds, letting her sweet honey coat me. She's so slick that I move against her with ease. I align myself with her entrance and gently spread her thighs farther, giving myself plenty of space. Staring into her eyes, I move forward, pressing the head against her entrance. I want this to be as painless as possible, even if I know it can't be completely.

I thrust forward a smidge, and a whimper escapes her lips. If she's afraid, she's wearing a brave face at the moment.

"You're so fucking beautiful," I whisper, leaning forward to pepper her chest with kisses. I move deeper inside her, her cunt tightening to the point of pain. "Fuck, Elena, I'm going to need you to relax a little. You're so tight. I'm afraid if I push inside you, I'll tear you."

I continue to kiss her, leaving a trail of wet kisses across her skin. They're enough to distract her, causing her to melt in my hands. As soon as I realize I can move again, I decide to slide deep inside. I wanted to take things slow, make it so I wouldn't hurt her as badly, but there is no easy way to claim someone's virginity. Using the remaining shreds of my self-control, I start to move.

Her gaze widens in what I can only imagine is surprise and

pain as I push through the thin barrier and fill her completely. Her nails dig into my shoulders deep enough I'm afraid they'll draw blood. Her beautiful features fill with pain, and she winces as I move.

"Shhh, everything is going to be okay. It'll take a little bit to adjust, but every time after this will be better."

I never imagined it would be this difficult to rein myself in, though. To keep from pounding her the way my body wants so much for me to do. Instead, I take her gently. I'm already so close to coming that my balls lift in preparation before I've lost my breath.

"Fuck, you're so tight and perfect!" I hiss through my teeth. "Tell me if I'm hurting you. My control is slipping, and I'm not sure how long I can hold on."

"Mm," she hums, and I respond by grinding a little on my next thrust, making her mouth fall open and her head roll from one side to the other.

I want to see her like this all the time, every day, for the rest of my life. How could I not?

"Keep doing that," she whispers with hope in her voice, so I do, driving her closer to the edge just as I drive myself there, too. Until we're both breathless and straining, and she's clutching me with arms, legs, and the increasingly tight muscles of her pussy.

"You're close," I whisper, propping myself on my forearms and thrusting faster. There's no helping it. "I can feel your little pussy quivering. Are you going to come for me?"

"Yes…" she whispers, clawing my shoulders. "Yes, I want you to come with me."

"I will, but I need you to come first," I growl, feeling the distinct flutter of her muscles. She's there, and I need to feel her pulsing around me.

"Oh god!" she moans and explodes a second later. Her pussy clenches all around me, and it's like heaven and hell colliding.

"Fucking shit!" I grit my teeth and strain and fight, but there's no holding it; there's no keeping it from rushing over me. That release, the relief of letting go.

She groans as I thrust harder and deeper, taking her a little rougher before filling her with the seed my grandfather is so interested in. Her pulsing muscles milk every drop as she rides out her orgasm, whimpering my name like a love song that grows softer until it's nothing but a long, deep sigh.

By the time I'm finished and pull back, the mixture of my cum and her virgin blood run down her crack and stain her thighs. I can't pretend the sight doesn't reach some deep, primal part of me and bring me pleasure beyond anything physical. I can't deny that part of myself any more than I can deny the guilt over her glowing face and the way she smiles. Like she's happy this happened.

And when her eyes open, I can't help but smile down at her, even as I curse myself for being too weak to resist her.

BEAST

25

ALICIA

*I*s this really happening? Is this my life? Waking up in Enzo's bed, where he pulls me in to hold me tight against him? And what about the fact that I don't really mind. What about how good it feels to be wrapped in his arms, his firm chest under my cheek? The slow, steady beating of his heart soothes me and almost lulls me back to sleep.

Almost.

There's still reality to contend with. Like the reality of how incredibly sore I am after last night. I knew he was big after seeing him naked, but it's a totally different story when he's hard.

Then there is the fact he was my first and that I'm not a virgin anymore. I'm not exactly thrilled that he's the one I lost it to, but at least he made sure I enjoyed myself. He took his time with me until I was practically begging for it.

The morning after, though, is another story. I never even got out of bed to clean myself up, thanks to the way I passed out soon after we both came, and now I'm wishing I had. When I manage to carefully unwind Enzo's arms to give myself some room, I look down between my legs and find dried blood on my inner thighs. Wonderful.

Getting out of bed is an experience. Not only do I feel a little twinge of pain with every step I take, but my legs are a little shaky, and my feet hurt after dancing for so long in those ridiculous—if sexy—shoes. I take one careful step after another, moving quietly across the room with the intention of using the bathroom in the hallway rather than Enzo's en suite bathroom.

But I stop when I hear voices at the foot of the stairs. There are men down there the way they've been for days now, even if I don't know why. Heightened security? I guess, but right now, they're seriously ruining my escape.

I could try creeping past the stairs to cross the hall, but there's a risk of them seeing me if they look up here. And I'm not exactly dressed. I pull back a little, closing the door softly before tiptoeing to Enzo's bathroom instead. I really don't want to wake him up, so this is pretty inconvenient, but he didn't so much as snort in his sleep when I got out of bed. Maybe I wore him out.

I catch sight of my little grin in the bathroom mirror and immediately frown at myself. There's nothing cute about this. "Get it together," I whisper while running a washcloth under warm water, then rub soap on it. I've already let things go way too far—not that I could have stopped him if he was really, truly determined to have sex last night, but I didn't have to be such a willing participant, either. Now he probably thinks I want him, or like this is going to be a normal occurrence, but it's not. It can't be.

Especially since he came inside me.

That can't happen again. Not only because I don't want to give that old man what he wants, but because I truly don't want to carry Enzo's child. I can't be tied to him like that, which is exactly what pregnancy would do. There would be no way of escaping this nightmare if we shared a child.

When I'm finished cleaning myself up and open the door, Enzo is still sound asleep. I have to force myself not to stare too long at him—he makes a beautiful sight, stretched out in bed, one arm flung over his head. His perfectly sculpted body is on display. Each muscle protrudes out, beckoning me to touch it. If I knew how to draw, I would sit down and sketch him for hours on end. His physical beauty is the kind of thing that should be captured and frozen in time.

All the more reason for me to get the hell out of this room as soon as possible. The longer I spend with him, the easier it is to forget how this all started. How he terrorized me and tortured me. This is not some lost soul in need of redemption.

I go to the door leading to the hallway and open it a crack, listening hard in case those men are still near the stairs. Dammit, they are. Their voices ring out, loud and clear, echoing up the stairwell. I glance over my shoulder to see whether they've woken Enzo, but it doesn't seem like they have.

"This whole thing is fucked," one of them grunts.

"No shit. But the old man has a plan in place, and you know there's no changing his mind."

The old man? Now I'm not annoyed. Instead, I'm interested, opening the door a little wider so I can hear them better. What are they talking about? I'm sure they're not feeling sorry for me in any way. I mean, my situation is fucked, but I doubt they have much sympathy. If they've thought of me at all.

"All we have to do is make sure Enzo and the girl steer clear. Everything else is going to work itself out. At least, that's what he says."

Steer clear of what? I'm so curious and concerned that I can almost forget modesty and stroll right out to the top of the stairs to ask them to elaborate.

Before I can do any such stupid thing, though, an arm snakes around my waist. I gasp, going stiff when Enzo pulls me against his chest.

"Sneaking away from me?" he murmurs, his lips brushing my earlobe. It causes a fluttering sensation in my core, and I can almost forget my soreness when he runs a hand over my hip and down my thigh.

"I wanted to get dressed," I whisper, "but I didn't want the guys down there to see me pass the top of the stairs."

"I like you better like this." He pulls me away from the door and closes it before bringing me back to the bed. "Plus, the thought of anyone else seeing you like this would make me irate, and I'd have to remove their eyes from their heads with a dull butter knife. I doubt you want to be responsible for someone else's death."

"Enzo..." I groan, trying to be playful when really, I'm trying to be strong. Sure, my overworked pussy is ready and willing to go for another round, but my brain is another story. This can't keep happening. I can't make this easy for him.

"That's right. I love it when you say my name. But I prefer hearing it when I'm between your legs." I have no choice but to sit down on the bed when he puts me there, then lie back as he lowers himself over me before planting hot, lingering kisses along my throat and chest. Every touch of his lips undoes me a little more, loosening the knots holding me together, ruining my resolve until I'm writhing and whimpering.

"I'm still so sore," I whisper, trying halfheartedly to make him stop. As if to prove it, he places a hand over my pussy, and I wince at the contact.

"You're also wet," he replies, grinning devilishly when I blush in embarrassment. "So something tells me you don't really mind it that much."

I'm never going to win, am I? He'll always have a way to come back at anything I try to use against him. All I can do is breathe deep as he parts my legs and looks down at what's between them.

He bites his lip, his nostrils flaring. "That's fucking insane." With one hand, he strokes himself, staring down at me while he hardens.

"What is?"

"You missed a few spots." He runs a finger over my sensitive flesh, and I gasp before sighing as the sweetest pleasure ripples through me. "It's on my cock, too. Your virgin blood."

"Oh, no, I'm sorry—" I try to sit up, but he places a firm hand against my chest, pushing me back.

"I didn't say you had to apologize. Seeing this is hot as fuck. Reminding me I'm the man who claimed your pussy first. Your virginity is mine, as all your other firsts will be."

He lowers himself onto his forearms and aligns himself with me. Pressing the head of his cock against me, he pushes inside, and I tense up, my nails digging into his shoulders. At the expense of causing me pain, he watches my face, encouraging me with praise, and takes it slow, inching his way inside, groaning once he's seated completely, and I can feel every bit of him. I hate myself for liking it so much. For craving it.

"Say it," he whispers in my ear, pulling back to fill me again. "Say it's mine, and nobody can ever have it."

"Yours. It's yours," I agree, my mouth falling open when he rolls his hips, and my body shivers at the delicious friction. His base rubs against my clit before he pulls back to do it again and again.

He props himself up on his palms, still working slowly, and I look down between us to watch his abs and shoulders work. I run my hands over them, marveling at how they move under his skin and the way they bunch and flex. As beautiful as he is when he's asleep, there's something almost miraculous about him now. I'm sure the heat building in my pussy with every slow, deliberate thrust has something to do with that.

"Is my cock going to make you come again?" he teases, his half-lidded eyes locking onto mine. "Look at me. I want you looking at me when you come. I want to watch."

Is there anybody who could resist something like that? And the deep, primal sensuality of his voice only pushes me closer to the edge. Watching him, feeling him, hearing him—it all builds up together until I'm helpless against it, riding a wave of sensation that starts to crest before I know what's happening.

"That's right," he grunts, his breathing faster now. "Tighten up for me, baby. Milk my cock. Take every drop. I don't want a drop wasted."

But should I? Is this right? Am I only going to end up regretting this? Those thoughts are quickly pushed aside when the tension finally breaks, and I gasp in surprise and pleasure as bliss washes over me, rippling through my arms and legs and every inch of my body.

"Good girl," he grunts, losing his rhythm and driving himself harder and faster until he throws his head back and goes still, growling through clenched teeth, his face flushing and tendons standing out on his neck before he finally collapses onto his forearms and rolls away.

I feel it, then. The wetness. His seed. It's on my thighs and dripping out of me. Dammit. What am I supposed to do? He can't keep coming inside me. Does the man have a problem with condoms or something? I know better than to bring it up. We've never discussed the use of protection, even though I know we should.

Maybe once we're married, I'll have a little more leeway. Maybe I can use Plan B or something like that when he refuses to pull out.

Because there is no way I'm going to be stuck in this insane family for the rest of my life. A baby with Enzo would be an end for me.

BEAST

26

ENZO

How does a man normally feel on his wedding day? I imagine he'd be nervous. It would be a good kind of nerves, though, wouldn't it? At least, if he was secure in the choice he'd made. If he knew the woman set to meet him at the altar was the right woman. The one woman he couldn't live without. Nerves would still be natural; fear of standing up in front of so many people, making a mistake, or dropping the ring. Something like that.

If he wasn't sure she was the right woman, though. It would be a whole other type of nervousness. Apprehension. Anxiety. A man might question everything about himself and everything about the chain of events that brought him to this moment. Standing in front of a mirror, wearing a new suit, minutes away from pledging his life to a stranger who hates him.

Because, of course, that's how this will turn out. She might have warmed up to me somewhat, but the underlying hatred is still there. Resentment I can't blame her for. I took her from her life without thinking. I was reacting. I was insulted and imagined I was taking it out on her father.

I had no idea I was forcing us both into an arrangement we couldn't back out of.

It doesn't matter now, does it? My motives. It changes nothing. After all, does a drunk driver's regret bring back the life of the person they killed in an accident? Even if she doesn't hate me the way she did at first, she's going to. A little more every single day she wakes up next to me, the symbol of how she lost all control over her life. The night she first looked into my eyes was the night she signed her life over.

The night I signed my life over, as well. I just didn't know it.

At least no one can ever say I didn't look my best today. A trip to the barber followed by a visit to the tailor to make sure everything was fitted properly have left me looking impeccable if I do say so myself. At least she'll have a husband who looks worthy of her when it comes time to stand together in front of that minister and tell a bunch of lies about being devoted to each other until death.

She deserves so much better than this. And there is the peril of allowing myself to get closer to her. Now that I know her better, there's no avoiding the truth: I am in no way the man she needs or deserves, but there's nothing we can do about it.

I have a duty to my family, my grandfather, whose voice rings out across the vast space downstairs as he requests drinks and food. He's in high spirits, finally on the verge of witnessing everything he's worked toward for years coming to fruition. I guess he can't be blamed for cracking jokes and taking bets on how soon it will be before my beautiful bride gives him a great-grandchild. He's not going to let that go, not that I would expect him to. I know him too well.

I'm sure she hears him, too, tucked away in the spare room as she prepares for what's to come. I'm sure Grandfather considered it an act of generosity, offering to hire people to come in and do her hair, makeup, and nails. The bride must be pampered, he insisted. She went along with it because she isn't a fool, though I could have told him she wasn't interested, that is, if he'd have listened. This act he's putting on is downright cruel at the heart of it. He knows she doesn't want this any more than I do, yet he makes a big show of pretending this is in any way normal.

It was also a test, and I know it even if he doesn't think I do. Making sure she's loyal, that she wouldn't hint to anybody at how unhappy she is about this arrangement. And she didn't because she's smart enough not to. How do I know that? Because I would have known otherwise. I would have known right away. Grandfather would have wasted no time telling me, perhaps even holding it over Alvarez's head, that his daughter was an unfaithful liability.

I know she's alone in there. Grandfather and Josef discussed the terms of the marriage contract earlier when the Alvarez family first arrived. But no one has been in to see Elena, not even her mother. There is so much about this family I don't understand and wish I did, considering the fact I'm marrying into them. Marriage means inheriting a spouse's family—especially in a marriage like this, where it was the family who arranged it in the first place. Controlling, manipulative, and self-serving.

Funny how the old superstition about a groom seeing his bride before the wedding tickles the back of my mind as I walk down the hall in her direction. What difference does it make if I see her now or not? This entire situation has been doomed from the beginning. For all I know, I might be improving our odds by tossing tradition out the window and visiting her before the ceremony. At the heart of it, tradition be damned—she deserves at least one person to check in with her before the ceremony, and if her parents can't be bothered, it will have to be me. It should be me.

I give the door a faint rap with my knuckles. "Can I come in? I only want to see you for a minute."

She doesn't hesitate. "Sure. Come in." Her voice isn't flat or empty in the way I would have expected—if anything, it's surprisingly light. The voice of a woman who sees no point in fighting anymore. A woman resigned to her fate. It makes me uneasy, but I open the door, prepared for whatever I find.

What I find is my bride sitting before a mirror, looking like an angel descended to earth. I already knew that dress was made for her, but the effect with the hair and the makeup and everything is overwhelming. Her upswept hairdo highlights the graceful lines of her neck, the way she holds her head high, so proud. Her already gorgeous face is breathtaking, thanks to a little skillfully applied makeup. She is every inch the beautiful bride.

And she's mine—though not really. There's a good chance she never will be. And now I understand what sits at the heart of my apprehension and misgivings.

I wish she had chosen me. I can't remember another time in my life when I felt this way. When I wanted to earn someone's trust and esteem. Not because of the family I belong to, not because she was ordered to. I want her to want me, Enzo, for myself.

I want her so deeply, so intensely, that it takes every scrap of self-control not to touch her now. I don't want her because of my family or because I'm supposed to. I want her because she's everything I can ever imagine wanting in a woman. Her beauty, her smarts, her kindness. That backbone of steel so cleverly concealed in what appears to be a weak, frail little body. She's ideal—perfect.

And she wants nothing to do with me, nor will she ever. I wouldn't know where to begin making her love me. And so it's with a heavy heart that I greet her—still, my sentiments are genuine. "There's never been a more beautiful bride, and there never will be."

She appears to give a startled little gasp as she turns away from the mirror, looking almost bewildered. "Thank you, but you don't have to say that."

"I mean it."

Is it that easy to make her happy? To say something kind to her? It almost doesn't seem fair that it would be that easy. Odds are she hasn't had many compliments given to her before now.

"You look very nice, as well."

I'm sure she means it, but I wave a dismissive hand, nonetheless. "It's much easier for a man." What do I say now? I hardly remember why I came down the hall, to begin with. My palms are sweating, and my heartbeat is erratic. What do I do now? How do I reach her? I can hardly believe this matters so much.

After a moment of uncomfortable silence, she offers, "I guess everything is pretty much ready to go? It sure sounds busy down there."

"Yes, but everything's under control. There's no rush. If you need another few minutes to get yourself ready, I can let everybody know."

She offers a brave, if shaky, smile. "Do you really think it will matter? Besides, I'm as ready now as I'm ever going to be. Another few minutes won't change anything."

This is all wrong, even worse than I imagined. I don't want her to sit there and take this the way she is. That's it. That's the problem. I want her to fight. I want her to care. The idea of her being broken and resigned leaves me feeling disappointed, conflicted, and even angry. What happened to her spirit? Is it all gone, used up? And all I'll have for the rest of my life is the empty shell of a woman I destroyed. Some men might be satisfied with that—in fact, I'm sure many in my world would, as it would mean one less headache to deal with. A pliant, timid little wife without the backbone to speak up for herself—especially one as beautiful as the woman seated before me—is essentially the jackpot.

Not for me. I can live with a lot of things—and I've had to, all the decisions I've made in my life—but I don't think I can bring myself to live with this. Knowing it was me who ruined her.

"Maybe you could—" I cut myself off before I can say anything idiotic like what was just about to fall from my lips. I was about to tell her to go, to run. To find a life of her own, far away from all of this.

For one brief, wild moment, her escape seems possible. I would take the fallout and accept all responsibility. I might even help her if she'd let me because she doesn't deserve this, and I'm not going to be the reason for her endless misery. It isn't fair to either of us.

"Ah, there you are!" As usual, Grandfather gets in the way, sneaking up on me out of nowhere and clapping me on the back before propelling himself into the room uninvited. He stops, his mouth falling open almost comically. He is truly playing it up today." Oh, what a beautiful bride. What a vision. You make an old man very happy, both of you."

"Thank you," she murmurs, averting her eyes. The way she

presses her lips together tells me she hasn't forgotten their conversation. There must have been more to it than he told me. Not that I didn't already know, but she's only confirmed it now.

"You're keeping everyone waiting," he tells us, looking back and forth. "I would never deny a bride and groom the chance to spend a few private moments together, but time is of the essence. The sooner we get through the ceremony, the sooner the two of you can spend all the time together you wish." There's no ignoring the knowing look he gives me. I'm almost embarrassed for him.

"Look at you," he says to me, hands on my shoulders, smiling from ear to ear. "I can hardly believe it. One day, you'll understand this feeling, looking at someone and suddenly realizing the years that have passed. Don't misunderstand me," he adds, throwing a smile Elena's way. "You know on the one hand, a child has grown into a man, but it's moments like this that make you realize you've still seen the child inside all this time. Now, there is no question. But as I say, you'll understand one day when your children grow."

He's about as subtle as a heart attack.

"Come on. Let's go." I don't want to subject her to more of this since she seems to shrink a little with every word he says. "Elena, we'll see you downstairs." I want to give her one last reassuring look, but she's staring down at her folded hands.

"Yes, your father will be up to see you momentarily," Grandfather adds before we leave the room, and he closes the door. Once we're in the hall, he claps me on the back. "A beautiful bride and a credit to you."

I force what I hope passes for a smile when what I want to do is shake him. This is too twisted, too sick. I didn't earn her. I didn't win her love. I took her, held her captive, and now neither of us has any choice in this. How am I supposed to be proud? How can he crow about it like he does? It's almost as if her presence has changed everything I thought I knew about myself, my family, and my life.

He leads me downstairs, then out to the yard. An archway has been assembled, covered in flowers, and a white runner leads from the back door to the place where the minister now stands. He's chatting with who I assume is Mrs. Alvarez, though I was not given the benefit of an introduction. She is petite and quiet, even a little spaced out. Is this what I have to look forward to? A shell of a woman sharing my bed?

Aside from that, guards are swarming the place, opposing sides eyeing each other, suspicious of one another. The tension in the air is enough to nauseate me, and for one moment, I almost wish my brother was here, if only to bulk up our side of things a bit, to appear stronger. Then again, I wouldn't want him to witness any of this shit. I hardly want to witness it myself. It's better for Christian to stay away. He can find out about this after the fact, along with the rest of the world.

At least Elena gets a sunny day for her wedding.

"Enzo, in these last few moments, I want to tell you how proud I am of you." We approach the end of the runner together, his hand firm against my lower back. Is he guiding me or pushing me? I can't tell. "You're stepping up like a man and doing what needs to be done for the good of the family. I need you to remember that's all that counts. That's all that ever matters, family. Making sacrifices for them. I have a lifetime of sacrifices to look back on, and I don't regret any of them. Even the ones that made me grit my teeth and shake my fist at God when the time came to make them."

We come to a stop, and he turns to me, holding me by the

arms, a look of fierce determination on his lined face. "My only wish, the only thing that matters to me in this life, is seeing you carry on the family name. That's all I need, all I want. Nothing else matters."

"That's what I intend to do," I reply since it's clear that's what he wants to hear. Yet there's more to it, and I can't pretend otherwise. I've never seen him like this, never heard him speak this way. Was he saving this speech for my wedding day, or is it off the cuff, a rare glimpse of emotion from an otherwise steely man? Whatever it is, I can't help but be moved, especially when he treats me to an impulsive hug. We are not huggers. I can probably count on one hand the number of times the man has embraced me, most of those times being in the days after I came to live with him.

"I'm very proud of you," he concludes. "I'm proud of the man you've become."

"Thank you, Grandfather." I can't say my heart is much lighter as we fall in place beside the minister, but at least I remember now why I'm doing this. For my family. Whether they deserve it or not.

And maybe, just maybe, Elena and I can find a way through this together.

At least, that's what I need to tell myself as I wait for her to join me.

BEAST

27

ALICIA

There it went. My last chance of getting out of this mess walked out the door. Not that I think it would've mattered what I said in these final moments before we exchanged vows. Neither of us has a choice here.

It doesn't matter how Enzo looked at me when he first entered the room or how electric the air was. I don't care that the softness and warmth in his eyes and smile cracked my heart open so he could find a way inside. This is wrong. It isn't what I want, and there's no hope of us being happy. At least, I won't be happy. I'm sure his life will go on however he wants it to, with no regard for what I want or need. Just because he was nice to me for a minute doesn't mean he'd be a good husband or even a willing one.

I can't let my heart run away from me. It will only hurt so much worse once the inevitable happens, and I'm left miserable, locked away forever while my husband makes the most of the deal our marriage cemented. I hope that wicked old man is happy with what he's forcing us into.

Though there did seem to be a little bit of genuine tenderness when he came in. I'm not imagining it—I wouldn't go out of my way to imagine a shred of humanity in a man who'd threaten to kill me if I don't get pregnant right away. I saw it; I heard it. He was happy to see us together the way a grandfather should be. He looked genuinely proud when he set eyes on Enzo, like for a minute they were family and nothing more. I hope that makes Enzo feel good after all the grief the guy has put him through.

Am I ever going to stop leading myself into caring about him? It's like I want to get myself hurt. Like I want to be disappointed and let down when my husband doesn't measure up to the image I've created in my loneliness.

I meet my gaze in the mirror and tighten my jaw in defiance. Fuck him. Fuck all of this. I'm doing what I need to do to survive, the way I always have. I'm not going to slink down the aisle with tears in my eyes. I won't beg anybody to let me out of it, either. And if he wants me to be his wife, he's going to see I'm no doormat. I'm not going to let any of these men break me down.

I'm taking one last look at myself in the mirror, touching up my makeup, when the door opens. It wouldn't be Enzo coming back already, would it?

No. It's a man I've never seen before, tall and dark-skinned and smiling like a shark. "There she is. My beautiful little girl."

I have to grit my teeth against a groan. I almost forgot about him. The man who's supposed to be my father, a man now sneering at me, just barely keeping it together when it's obvious he wants to laugh. I've heard his name used before. Alvarez.

"I never thought this day would come," he adds with a snicker. Obviously, this is all incredibly hilarious to him.

Then I guess it would be. He's getting a deal out of this, but

I'm not even his daughter. Instead of barging in and demanding to hear the whole story from my point of view, he's laughingly going along with it. "Why didn't you tell them the truth from the beginning?" I whisper. "Please, I'm trying to understand."

Like magic, his smile dissolves into something more sinister, something that goes with those cold, dead eyes of his. "Who says you get to understand anything? You're the one who used my family name. I'm the one who deserves an explanation—not that I care much about you or your reason for doing anything."

I can't help but gasp at the sight of the gun he pulls out from his waistband, scrambling backward until I hit the vanity table. He points it at me, his handsome face cold and hard. "Where's the product you stole? Don't pretend you don't know what I'm talking about."

That's all he cares about? I should've known. I mean, why would he give a shit about me, anyway? "I don't know! I really don't."

He advances on me, one slow step at a time. "Don't lie to me. There might be a minister waiting outside and twenty guards wandering around, but I could kill you right now, and I wouldn't feel a thing."

I have no trouble believing that. I thought Enzo was bad? There is no life behind this man's eyes. I can't stop bouncing my attention between them and the gleaming pistol aimed at my chest. "I'm telling the truth. I don't know what happened to it. And I wasn't trying to steal it, either. I was supposed to deliver it."

"I don't want to hear your shit," he barks with a wave of the gun, which he quickly aims again. "You're going to give me what I'm looking for, or this white dress is going to turn red real fast."

I don't know what to do. It's just like when Enzo first took me. The way he insisted on ignoring everything I said, so sure I was lying to him all the time. This feels like I'm in that nightmare all over again.

His eyes dart over my face, his jaw twitching. "Well? What's it going to be? And let me tell you something, whatever your name is: nobody steals from me and walks away. Ask anybody, and they'll tell you. I'm not a man who takes theft lightly."

When he falls silent, I whisper, "I'm sure you aren't." After all, it seems like he's waiting for something.

"So the fact that I'm even giving you a chance to tell me the truth says a lot." His mouth twists in a nasty smirk. "But it should also tell you I'm not used to controlling myself when I've been betrayed. So I wouldn't rely on kindness much longer."

"I completely understand what you're saying," I whisper, praying nobody is standing right outside the door. Granted, I'm screwed either way, but if I'm going to die, I would rather it be quick, the way my supposed father is threatening. Something tells me Enzo wouldn't make it quick.

All I can do is shrug helplessly. "I know you won't believe this, but I would tell you if I knew. I really would."

"So you're going to go through with this marriage? Even though it's all a lie?"

It's a ridiculous question, but it goes to show how little this man understands my situation. He's so busy worrying about himself, he hasn't given me a moment's thought—what a surprise. "What choice do I have? From the beginning, he was so sure I was a part of your family. I never said I was. He just assumed. No matter what I told him, he wouldn't listen—any more than you'll listen now," I add because what the hell? I have nothing left to lose at this point.

He scowls, eyes narrowing. Would he seriously shoot me here in this house, with everybody waiting for us? Not that I think he would particularly care about our surroundings, but there are guards everywhere, waiting for him to walk me down the aisle. I'm sure everybody saw him walking in here, too. It's not the kind of situation he could escape easily.

Once I look at it that way, I have the courage to lift my chin a little higher. "I don't want to do this, but at least you made it possible for me to keep my life when you didn't expose me. I guess I should thank you for that."

"I didn't do it for you," he growls, looking toward the door over his shoulder before turning back to me. "Last chance. We both know you don't want to do this. Tell me where the package is, and I'll see to it you get out of here. I'll take care of everything. You'll be free and never have to see any of us again. But I need that damn package."

I could weep. I honestly could. Not because I believe he would actually set me free. Men like him don't keep big promises like that to people like me. He thinks I'm a thief. Why would he let me go? As soon as he had what he wanted, I'd be dead.

But then I'm dead either way, aren't I? And I have been from the beginning. Anything else I've told myself was a lie, an illusion I only wanted to be true. My hopes of escape, all of it. One fairy tale after another.

"I would tell you if I knew," I whisper, my voice trembling with emotion I can't hide. "And I am sorry. Really. I never wanted to get mixed up in all this."

He stopped listening as soon as I turned him down. "Very well. That's what you want? You just dug your own grave." He hides the gun again before grabbing me by the elbow and dragging me toward the door. "Then we'd better get you out there. Your loving groom is waiting."

"What are you going to do?" I whisper in terror once we reach the hall. It's empty, but guards wait at the foot of the stairs.

"I guess we'll have to wait and see, won't we?"

"Are you going to tell them?" He only responds with a nasty little grin that turns my stomach and brings tears to my eyes. I've never felt so completely alone and friendless in my entire life. I'm at the mercy of this maniac.

Then he flips a switch inside himself and turns into a doting father. I'm not sure which version of him scares me more. "Let's go, sweetheart," he murmurs as we descend the stairs. "It's time to get you married off."

I force a smile, but it's weak and teary. Well, don't brides sometimes cry?

He walks me through the house and out through the side door to the yard. It's simple, the setup, but strangely touching just the same. A single row of chairs sit at the end of a long, white runner, and at the far end stands an archway decorated with flowers.

On one side, where the bride's family normally sits, there's a dark-haired woman dressed and groomed beautifully, immaculate from head to toe. Is she supposed to be my mother? Something about the sight of her is enough to make me want to weep more than ever before. Both sides are pulling out all the stops to make this look legitimate. I wonder what my so-called father did to convince his wife to sit there like that and live out this lie.

Is Enzo going to have to talk me into something like this one day? Does she ever get to make her own choices? She won't look at me, staring at her folded hands once she stands at the minister's instruction.

On the other side, there's a man dressed in black, who I vaguely recognize as one of Enzo's grandfather's guards. I remember him from that uncomfortable conversation in the kitchen, all of which he witnessed. He's sitting directly in front of where good old Grandad is standing behind Enzo like he has to be close to his boss at all times.

We come to a stop at the end of the aisle, and the evil man at my side tucks my hand around his elbow. "Here we go. You'll wish you had come clean with me by the time this is over."

I wish the man would understand that I was already coming clean. What is it with these guys? Why do they find it impossible to listen to the truth? I guess it's because the truth isn't what they want to hear, not really. It doesn't align with their purposes, so they want to ignore it like they can twist things however they want them.

Shit. This is happening. There's no stopping it. My whole life flashes before my eyes while I weigh my options and find, once again, that there are none. Either Alvarez tells the truth when we reach the altar, and I have no doubt Enzo would put a bullet in my head in front of the minister and everybody in attendance.

Or he'll go along with it, and I'm screwed anyway. Tied in marriage to a man I don't really know and will never understand. No matter how I look at it, this is a shit sandwich. There's no prettying it up.

Then Enzo smiles at me from where he's waiting in front of the makeshift altar, and a very tiny part of me responds warmly, happily. It's like he almost wants to be here, like he almost wants it to be me walking down the aisle. It's so unfair. I can't even completely dread saying my vows because something tells me that if we were left alone to live our lives in peace and privacy, we might actually end up being happy together. Without all these other influences and his grandfather in his ear all the time. Without him feeling like he has to show off or do the whole performative alpha male thing. If given the chance, I might actually end up liking him. Even loving him.

But there won't be any such chance because that's not the way life goes. At least not my life.

I draw a deep breath that does nothing to calm my nerves.

Time to get this over with.

28

ENZO

My god, she's exquisite, floating down the aisle on her father's arm. From the corner of my eye, I see him smiling from ear to ear, teeth gleaming in the sunlight, but the bulk of my attention is focused on his daughter.

I don't care if it makes me look weak or besotted. I can't take my eyes off her, drinking in every detail of the way her body looks in that dress and how she seems to float in it. I wonder how quickly we can get this whole ceremony over with. I would much rather have a repeat of our time in the dressing room, only this time, I won't stop at eating her out. We're far past that point now.

She barely meets my gaze, for the most part, staring straight ahead. Her eyes brush over her mother, but they dart away before she makes any meaningful eye contact. No doubt she feels just as betrayed by her as she does by her father, whose chest is puffed out so far I'm surprised his jacket can stay buttoned. I can't imagine the sort of pain it must cause both women, knowing they have no control over anything happening today. Does Mrs. Alvarez see herself in her daughter? Does Elena see her future in her quiet, empty mother?

We can create our own future, can't we? It doesn't have to be that way for us. Why didn't I tell her that upstairs? I should have. I should have told her we can make this work somehow together. That even though neither of us chose this, we can choose a future of our own. We can break the cycle and set our own path. It doesn't have to be hopeless.

I'll have to wait to tell her all of that after the ceremony. I wish I could have given her that bit of extra encouragement beforehand.

When they reach me, Josef turns to his daughter and gives her a big, smacking kiss on the cheek. She recoils from him, and all I want is to take hold of her and tell her she never has to see him again if she doesn't want to. That I understand if she hates him. Starting today, we're going to make things right.

When I make a move toward her, prepared to get between them, she gives me a wide-eyed look and takes hold of my arm. Silently, she turns me toward the minister and stands beside me, her chin lifted, her eyes staring straight ahead. She's in a hurry to get this over with. I imagined she would cry, perhaps beg one last time to stop this. Now, it almost seems like she's eager. I can only imagine her father reminded her of all the reasons this is necessary—and I don't want to think about what he might have threatened her with up there when they were alone. I might have to kill him.

I understand why she would recoil from him when I look at it that way. He's acting like this is all a big show, like something about all of this is amusing, while I have no doubt he threatened her with no less than murder if she doesn't go through with this charade.

He backs away, standing beside his wife, and I turn my attention away from them and focus on Elena again. A light breeze teases strands from her elaborate hairstyle, framing her face. A face that is now a stony mask, the expression of someone who knows what must be done no matter how she feels about it. I should have said something more to her. I should have given her something to hold on to while she was no doubt being threatened by Josef. I'm going to find a way to make this up to her. I have to. I don't know that I'll be able to live with myself if I don't.

"Dearly beloved," the minister begins, an older man who smiles at both of us in a gentle, understanding sort of way. "We are gathered together to celebrate the union of these two souls. If there is anyone in attendance who believes they should not be united in marriage, let them speak now."

When Grandfather chuckles at my right hand, I turn to him in surprise. "We're past that point."

Elena's sharp intake of breath tells me she doesn't appreciate the joke.

"Very well." Still, the minister looks back and forth between her and me, almost as if he's expecting one of us to protest. When neither of us does, he nods.

It's the strangest feeling, this sense of both being in a dream and in reality. I understand now when she described an out-of-control train she knows is going to derail. I can relate, too. Even if I refused right now, the outcome would be violent. Even tragic. It would mean a declaration of war between the families, and how many lives would be lost as a result of that? How many of our people and theirs would be sacrificed? It brings to mind Grandfather's description of gritting his teeth and shaking his fist at God.

I want to do that right now, but it wouldn't make a difference. None of it would. I would still end up destroying my family. When I think about it that way, it seems only natural and wise to go along with this. It's the responsible thing to do, no matter how much I hate knowing what this is doing to her.

I find her hand close to mine and catch her fingers, giving them the briefest, slightest bit of pressure. *I'm here. I'm here with you. We're in this together. I'm sorry for all of this. Sorry I ever took you. Sorry I hurt you, and sorry I'm hurting you now. I'll find some way to make this up to you. I will take away the pain and rage and helplessness you feel right now and replace it with something better.* Even if I was allowed to speak to her freely, I know the words would stick in my throat. I've never felt this useless.

"Will the two of you please turn to face each other?" We do as the minister instructs, then join our hands. Hers tremble, and I hold them tight, hoping against hope that some of my strength can go to her. She's staring at my chin, refusing to meet my gaze. There's no light in her eyes, either. The man needs to get through this ceremony fast because I'm not sure how much more I can take of watching her die a little bit with every passing moment.

"Enzo De Luca, do you take this woman to be your lawfully wedded wife?" Everything else he says fades into the background of my consciousness, the blood rushing in my ears drowning out the sound of his voice. My lawfully wedded wife. My wife. The mother of my children, eventually. What kind of mother will she be to them? I imagine she'll love them because they come from her, but will her feelings toward me hurt them in some way? I have to protect her. Above all else, I have to keep her safe. I can't let her end up the way my mother did—though the fact that she died at my father's hand means we are already ahead of the game since I have no intention of ever doing to Elena what he did to my mother. His own wife, the mother of his children. I doubt I'd understand any better than I do now if he explained his intentions and reasoning to me.

But that won't be her. This might have started off in the worst possible way, but it doesn't have to end that way.

The minister falls silent, and I realize it's my turn to speak. What did he say? I'm supposed to say I do, aren't I? Grandfather even nudges me, and I have to grit back the impulse to tell him to back the hell off. "I do," I murmur instead, hoping against hope she'll look me in the eye. She doesn't, doesn't even give any indication she heard me. She's that checked out.

"And you, Elena—"

"I do," she whispers.

Grandfather chuckles while Josef lets out a booming laugh. "Eager," he points out, laughing again.

No, she just wants to get it over with.

The minister clears his throat, his cheeks going red. "You have to at least let me earn my fee and finish what I had to say," he explains, much to Josef's amusement. "As I was saying, do you take this man to be your lawfully wedded husband?"

I squeeze her hands as he continues, willing her to look at me. This time she does, her eyes meeting mine for the first time since this started, and I offer her the warmest smile I can muster. I'm sure it's a little sad, as well, because this is a rather sad situation. If she could only understand I'm right here with her, she might be able to get through this in less pain than she's in now.

Finally, the minister finishes his spiel, and she nods slowly, eyes locked with mine. "I do."

I smile again, and this time her lips stir. A good sign. I'm not naïve. We'll still have a long way to go, but now at least, I have a glimmer of hope.

My god. Have I fallen for this woman? If I haven't, I'm certainly in the process of it. Never in my life have I cared so deeply about the feelings of another—all the evidence is there. How it pains me to think of her in pain. My guilt over this entire situation, the fact that I was willing for a moment to call this off so she could flee. Even knowing the turmoil that would cause, I was willing to let her do it because she means more to me than even my grandfather's wishes. More than even my family. I would rather her be happy or at least free.

"Do we have the rings?"

Grandfather taps me on the shoulder and holds out the open box containing matching platinum bands. We weren't even given the chance to choose our wedding rings. I'll make that up to her, as well. I'll make it all up to her. For now, I take the smaller of the two rings and slide it over her finger while repeating the words the minister feeds me. When it's her turn, she does the same, this time looking me in the eye while her lips twitch slightly in the beginnings of a smile. It's encouraging enough to lighten the pressure in my chest. And gives me hope that we can find a way through this together as a team. We might have been forced into it, but we can make the best of it so long as she's willing to try. I know we can. I can hardly wait to tell her all of this, though I know it will be agony trying to put words to what I'm feeling.

I wonder how a so-called man of God can smile so wide and genuinely as he places his hands on top of ours. "Then, by the power vested in me, I pronounce you husband and wife. Enzo, you may kiss your lovely bride."

I'd like to do a lot more than kiss her. For starters, I would like to take off her garter with my teeth—that is, if she's wearing one. I'd be happy to settle for her underwear if not.

I draw her closer, prepared to seal the agreement with a kiss.

Until a familiar sound splits the air around us. Sharp, sudden, and out of place. The crack of a single gunshot.

Instinct makes me throw myself over her, and we crash to the ground as chaos erupts around us.

BEAST

29

ALICIA

It all happened so fast.

One second, we were wrapping things up with me in a daze the whole time, waiting for the moment Alvarez would announce I'm not his daughter and this was all nothing but a sham. Holding my breath, I'm expecting it to come at any moment, but it didn't. We were moments away from the final kiss to seal the deal.

The next, it sounded like firecrackers going off. That's what I thought the noise was at first, that Enzo's grandfather had ordered a display or something and it was going off too early. My poor, overwrought brain couldn't keep up with what was happening.

Then I was on the ground, where I still am, with Enzo on top of me. From where I'm lying, all I can see are feet pounding the grass as guards run in every direction.

Think, think! Am I in pain? I check in with my body, but there doesn't seem to be pain coming from anywhere except from where my ass hit the ground. My ribs aren't holding up so well under Enzo's weight, either. I don't think I was hit by a bullet, though.

Then my heart seizes, and I place my hands against Enzo's shoulders, trying to push him off me so I can check him over. What if I only thought he was protecting me, but he really fell against me because he was hit? "Enzo?"

He's not moving, his weight crushing me. "Enzo!" I manage to choke out, finally driving my knee into his ribs hard enough that he pays attention.

He pushes himself up and looks down at me, scanning my face, running his fingers over my cheek and down my throat. "Were you hit? Are you injured?" His pinched expression hinting at fear.

"I'm fine," I whisper, relief wrapping a hand around my heart and squeezing tight. "What about you?" I run my hands over his chest, but everything's normal, his shirt clear of blood.

"I'm fine, too." He's all right. He didn't get hurt. I can't believe how much better that makes me feel. I could've lost him. I don't want to lose him. Oh god, am I in love with this man?

Fear hardens, becoming rage. "What the hell was that?" he barks, looking around. He begins getting up, straightening himself out, and I'm about to do the same—that is, until he lets out a choked moan. The sound of it rips through me and threatens to break my heart. I look around, trying to find what he's reacting to.

It doesn't take long. "Grandfather!" he shouts, but there's no response from the old man now lying flat on his back, arms and legs splayed out. Enzo gets up and pulls me along with him, even though I'm not on my feet yet. I end up sliding across the grass, but he's not paying attention.

He's too busy shouting at his grandfather, falling to his knees at the man's side. "No, no, please," he whispers, taking the old man's face in his hands and patting his cheeks. "Come on. Don't do this. Don't leave me."

I don't have the heart to tell him it's already done.

"Somebody, help him!" Enzo turns to me, his eyes wild. "Do something! You did it for Prince! Please, help him!" His voice breaks toward the end, and that might be the saddest part of all of this. How broken he is.

But it's obvious there's nothing I can do. I take his hand, wrapping both of mine around it. "I'm so sorry," I whisper. "But he's already gone. There's nothing I can do." The man's got a hole in his chest, and his eyes are wide open, staring up at the blue sky. He was probably killed instantly. This is nothing like Prince.

"But you have to," Enzo grits out, squeezing my hand until I cry out in pain. "You have to!"

"I can't! I'm sorry, but he's already gone. Look at him." I nod toward him. "I'm sure it was instantaneous. He didn't feel a thing."

Meanwhile, chaos is still unfolding all around us. The minister has run off along with Mrs. Alvarez, both of them ducking for cover. Guards are still swarming the grounds, shouting at each other.

But right now, the only thing in the world is Enzo, who pulls me to my feet and throws an arm over my chest before pressing a gun to my temple. It's ridiculous, but all I can think is I'm about to be part of the world's shortest marriage.

"I'll fucking kill her!" he barks at Alvarez, who has barely moved since everything fell apart. "You did this! This was all your plan!"

Alvarez holds up his hands, shaking his head. "No, this wasn't me. I had nothing to do with it."

"You're fucking lying!" I hear how uneven Enzo's voice is. How much emotion is in it. How close to the edge he's come. This man was the only family he had, and while he was a pain in the ass, there had to be a lot of love there. Now he's lost everybody who loved him.

"Enzo, please!" I wail, pulling at the arm pressed tight to my chest in hopes of making him release me. It doesn't matter. He's not letting go. He's never letting go. Not when he's convinced I'm the enemy who wouldn't save his grandfather's life.

"So this was the plan all along. I should have fucking known!"

"That's not true!" All that earns me is the gun pushed tighter against my temple.

Alvarez looks around, waving his hands like he's signaling for things to calm down. "Enzo, you need to stop. Think. What would I have to gain by setting this up?"

"Listen to him!" I plead.

"This wasn't my plan. Okay? You need to settle down before you do something you're going to regret."

My eyes dart around, taking in the full scene. Men from both sides point guns at each other, at Enzo, at me. The wind could blow the wrong way, and we'd all be dead. It's that tense. I'm afraid to breathe.

"Enzo, please listen," I beg, on the verge of tears. "Let me go. I didn't do anything. I wish I could've helped him. I really do."

"Shut up," he growls, his arm almost crushing me. "You've already said too damn much, and I was stupid to listen to a single word."

Yes, we might be happy if the rest of the world would leave us alone. Sadly, that's never going to happen. Especially not in this world, where a wedding can turn into a bloodbath at the drop of a hat.

Now, Enzo and I are back to square one, with me waiting for him to end my life.

BEAST

30

ENZO

And nd here we are, back to where we started. With her fighting against me, clawing at my arm, choking on her tears. Thinking if she just fights hard enough, she'll be free. She still hasn't learned.

"Enzo, please," she begs, blubbering all over the place. Trying her damnedest to fuck with my head the way she's fucked with me all this time.

"No wonder you were in such a hurry to get this over with," I hiss in her ear, and for one wild moment, I imagined biting it, listening to her scream in pain as her blood dripped onto the dress she had the nerve to put on. "So this is what the two of you talked about while you were alone, is it? You always knew this was going to happen. Isn't that right?"

"No!" she bawls. "No, I swear! I didn't know about any of this!"

"More lies. I'm supposed to trust you? Knowing where you come from?" What a fool I've been. Standing here, thinking all these ridiculous thoughts about our future, about how I want to make this better for her, how I want to make her happy. I lost all sense of reality, and it's all thanks to her. I stopped thinking of her as my hostage and started thinking of her as an equal. The biggest mistake I ever could have made.

A mistake that left my grandfather dead at my side, staring blindly up at the sky. My grandfather. The strongest man I ever knew, who I now realize I never imagined leaving me. How am I supposed to get through any of this without him? How am I supposed to take over the family after this?

Of course, that would be another of Josef's plans, wouldn't it? I press the gun tight against her head, and she lets out a full-bodied howl like an animal caught in a trap. And that's exactly what she is. A lying, deceitful little animal. "It should be you I'm pointing this at," I growl at Alvarez, still standing with his hands raised. "This is all you. You set this in motion. You deserve to die."

"I'm telling you, this wasn't me."

"Will you please listen to him," she begs, almost choking on her tears. "Please!"

"Shut up," I growl. "I've heard enough of your bullshit lies. Do you think I would believe a word you say now? And there I was, feeling sorry for you. Wanting to make this up to you. What a fucking joke. You're nothing but a lying little snake. I blame myself for forgetting that."

Alvarez hasn't made a move, choosing to simply stare at me. No threats of what awaits me if I harm his precious daughter. He hardly looks at Elena at all. "Are you sure this wasn't a plan on your end?" he shouts. "A way to negate our deal? Because guess what, boy? It's sealed. Cemented. The old man signed his name on the line. There's nothing you can do about it."

"Then how about I fucking kill her since nothing I do will affect our deal? What about that? Will you be standing there looking so smug when I put a bullet in her brain?" She whimpers pitifully, but all that does is make me tighten my hold on her. The lying, traitorous little bitch. I can't believe I let myself fall for her tricks. There's a mistake I'll never make again.

He lowers his brow, smirking. "So you're going to kill her? Your own wife? Because that's what she is now, boy."

"Call me boy one more time," I warn in a growl. "See how well that goes for you."

"You and I both know damn well that if you so much as gesture at me with that piece of yours, you're done. Dead on the spot, just like the old man. And what would happen to your precious little family then? How many people will move in to claim what he fought for all this time? Sort of seems like a waste, doesn't it?"

"Enough talk. You're only trying to save your own ass." But at the same time, I know every word of it is true. I wouldn't even have time to aim at the man before one of the half dozen or so men now training their guns on me opened fire. They would turn me into a corpse on the spot, I have no doubt.

Except for one thing. "You'd have your men open fire on me while I have her in front of me like this? Your bluff is showing. You aren't even very good at it, are you?"

That's when the most chilling thing of all happens. That's when he smiles the way he did when he brought Elena to my side. The way he did back at the restaurant when his demeanor struck me as slightly strange. A man who knows he's been bested does not smile that way.

"Oh no," he murmurs, touching a hand to his chest. "You're going to threaten me with the death of my sweet little girl? As it has been from the beginning, the joke's on you. I've already been through that."

Elena's broken sobs barely register on my overworked

brain. As usual, the man has found a way to leave me at a loss. "And what is that supposed to mean?"

"It means my daughter is dead. She died years ago, my Elena. We never told anyone because it was no one's business. This little bitch?" He waves a dismissive hand, scoffing. "She's not mine. Not my blood. I didn't even adopt her."

"That's not true," I grunt.

"Isn't it?" he sneers. "I don't know why she used my daughter's name, but she's no daughter of mine. In fact, when I met up with her upstairs? That was the first time I ever set eyes on her."

It's the strangest thing. I heard what he said, every word spoken loud and clear. Yet it doesn't make sense, almost like he lapsed into a different language, one I don't understand. Because there is no way I heard what I think I heard. I must have mistaken him.

"You're lying," I scoff.

He tips his head to the side. "You don't really think I'm lying, do you? No, you look like a scared little boy who finally figured out how badly he fucked himself over." His smile is triumphant as he goes about re-buttoning his jacket, then using both hands to slick down his hair. "She's not mine. She never was. You assumed she was. Didn't anybody tell you what happens when you assume things? Or are you so young that you haven't had time to learn that lesson yet?"

He offers an amused little shrug. "Now you know. I like to think I helped school you a little."

"You're a lying bastard."

"I admit, I have lied in my life, and I have been called a bastard. Maybe I am," he admits with a laugh. "But I'm completely serious now." All semblance of good humor drops from his face when he scowls. "She's not mine. But you know what is mine? Everything your grandfather signed over to me today. I don't know who killed him—that's the truth—but before they did, he made me a very happy man."

Then because this entire situation could not be more bizarre, he begins backing away. "I don't care what happens to her," he says with a shrug. "She's nothing to me. But congratulations on the wedding." He is most of the way inside the house, where his wife waits by the door, before he gestures for his men to follow him. They smirk and sneer but follow his instructions, though they keep their guns trained on me for as long as he and his wife are visible.

I don't know what to do. What comes next? My entire life and everything I thought was true just came crashing down around me. My grandfather is dead, and my family is now in shambles. Josef Alvarez has made a fool of us all, thanks in no small part to an assumption I made that he was more than willing to allow me to continue believing. He must have seen all of this from the beginning. The moment he learned what happened in the warehouse. Who told him? I don't know. I only know that men like him have no trouble piecing together how a situation will benefit them. Right away, he saw what needed to be done. If she wasn't going to tell me the truth, if only to save her own hide, he would continue to bluff until the very end. Until his family was bound to mine, thanks to a contract I was never even given the privilege of seeing.

And now I'm holding a woman in front of me like a shield, but she's not the woman I thought she was. The woman I talked myself into believing she was. No matter how long I live, I will never find a way to stop hating myself for what I let her do to me. The fool I let her make of me. The fool I've made of myself.

"Well, Enzo, please—"

I clamp my hand over her mouth, cutting her off. There's one thing I know for sure. "I don't want to hear a word from your lying lips again. Whoever you are, you are nothing to me, and I'll see to it you pay for everything you've done."

Her tears roll over the back of my hand, but I ignore them because they're probably all for show. Just as they always were.

"I should have killed you," I whisper in her ear, relishing the way she shudders, the muffled sounds of her sobs. "You are going to pay for this. If it takes years, I'm going to see to it that you pay."

And then, because I can't stand being this close to her, I shove her in the direction of the nearest guard. "Get her upstairs. Lock her in the bedroom. I'll deal with her later."

"No, please!" she screams as he takes hold of her. She trips over her dress, and I hear it ripping, and the sound pleases me. She doesn't deserve to wear it. "Enzo, please, you know this isn't right!"

"Don't you say a fucking word to me about what's right and what isn't," I snap. "Don't you say another word to me unless you're answering a direct question, you scheming little bitch."

"But I love you! I love you! Don't do this!"

I hold up a hand, and they come to a stop while I walk slowly toward them. She's shaking, tearstained, her hair hanging in tangles around her face, Grandfather's blood on her dress. My grandfather's blood. My family's blood.

"If I believed you—which I don't, by the way—it wouldn't matter," I inform her. "Do you want to know the saddest part about all of this? So sad, it's almost funny?"

She shakes her head, quietly sobbing, tears dripping onto her tits. I should have carved them up when I had the chance.

"I love you, too." Hope washes over her face, lighting up her eyes. "But I'm going to have to kill you, anyway."

I take dark, twisted pleasure in the broken sob that tears its way from her a moment before I nod, signaling her removal from my presence. The sound of her heartbreak is a twisted symphony that plays in my head long after the sound fades away.

Leaving me standing alone with my grandfather's body and my family's entire future on my shoulders.

∼

Continue this series with Savage Vow

About J.L. Beck

J.L. BECK IS A **USA TODAY** AND INTERNATIONAL BESTSELLING AUTHOR AND ONE HALF OF THE AUTHOR DUO BECK & HALLMAN.

WHEN SHE ISN'T WRITING YOU CAN FIND HER SITTING WITH A CUP OF COFFEE, IN A COMFY CHAIR, WITH A BOOK IN HAND. SHE'S A MOM (BOTH KIDS AND PUPS), WIFE, AND INTROVERT.

LEARN MORE ABOUT HER BOOKS ON HER WEBSITE

WWW.BLEEDINGHEARTROMANCE.COM

About S. Rena

S. Rena (Sade Rena) is a *USA Today* bestselling author of dark contemporary and dark paranormal romance.

As with her contemporary titles, Sade enjoys spinning tales that are angsty, emotional, and sexy. But because she loves a villain just as much as she loves a hero, she also writes dark, diverse characters who are flawed and morally grey.

Visit www.saderena.com

Printed in Great Britain
by Amazon